THE LAST WINTER

THE
LAST WINTER

WRITTEN AND ILLUSTRATED BY
SAMWISE DIDIER

INSIGHT ◉ EDITIONS

San Rafael, California

CHAPTER 1

THE MARCH OF THE GIANTS

MASSIVE THUNDERHEADS CRACKED in the northern skies of Icegard. Snow and hail fell upon the world in a blanket of ghostly oblivion. The great oceans froze and turned from violent waves to jagged sheets of green ice. Lord Wintyr, the greatest of the frost giants, raised his axe, and the roar of a thousand fiends of Icegard echoed into the pale, frozen night.

Far to the south, a hellish glow lit the skies of Firehome. Volcanoes erupted, spitting fiery ash into the atmosphere. King Sumyr, the ruler of the fire giants, held high his black iron sword, and it ignited with a burst of crimson flame. War horns blared, and a choir born of a thousand beasts of fire resounded into the blackened dawn.

The brothers of frost and fire marched forth from their realms with death and vengeance in their hearts. Each army had but one destination in mind—the island of Mistgard. Their goal was its annihilation.

***

Though surrounded by roaring chaos, the island of Mistgard lay in somber silence. No fires lit the hearths, and no songs filled the dens. All of the

great lodges stood empty. Those missing from the halls were known as the Pandyr, and all Pandyr, from chieftain to warrior, from young to old, congregated in the Circle in the Sky. The Circle was an old burial ground perched high upon the windswept cliffs of Mistgard, and it was here that the clans would gather to honor their ancestors and return them to the earth. Surrounded by tall obelisks of gray and brown granite, the Pandyr clans stood grimly as the sleet and ash started to fall, and if they felt the chill or burn, they did not show it.

The eight clans had not gathered together in such numbers for many years. Feuds and clan wars had gone unchecked for generations, fragmenting

a once-united people into separate factions. But today, the rival clans put aside their grudges to pay their final respects to the mother of all the clans. On this day, Sprign, the Den Mother, the benevolent giantess who created the first of all Pandyr ages and ages ago, would be laid to rest.

Legends told that before time began, there were only the great Skulls in the Sky. They floated through the endless astral oceans and grew lonely amidst the stars. They chose to join with each other, and when they aligned, life was born. To this life they gave a name: Sprign, the Dawn of Creation. They watched Sprign and placed her upon a barren world, where she claimed a small area of the realm and created the mountainous island of Mistgard. She was the living avatar of the land, the sky, and all of their beings.

The Pandyr, the flora, and the fauna were all her children, and to all of her offspring Sprign gave two gifts: life and the will to live it as they would. Some beasts grazed while others survived by the hunt. The Pandyr, her most evolved creations, farmed the land, foraged the hills, and found sustenance among the mountains and in the waters surrounding the island. All of Sprign's children contributed to the perfect symmetry of existence upon the isle of Mistgard.

Soon after the creation of Sprign, the giant Sumyr, the Son of Fire, strode forth. As Sprign created Mistgard, Sumyr took a large area to the south,

shaped the realm of Firehome, and filled it with foul, burning beings of ash, fire, and obsidian.

Following Sumyr came the Silent Son, the stone giant Fell. Whereas Sumyr was rash, Fell was somber. Unlike Sumyr, Fell had a strong bond with Sprign, and he chose to create his kingdom beneath that of his sister, calling it the Under Realm.

After the birth of Fell came the largest and most powerful of giants: the Bringer of the End, the frost giant Wintyr. He seized the remaining areas of the world and spawned the frozen lands known as Icegard, which he filled with abominable beasts born of ice and bone. Wintyr looked to the heavens

and belched forth storms and hate toward his creators. The Skulls in the Sky grew fearful and separated, never to join again. Returning to the high heavens, the Skulls in the Sky left their children to wander the newly born world alone.

All of the giants ruled over their realms. While Sprign gave her children free will, the other giants subjugated their creations to have no will other than that of their creators.

Firehome and Icegard were bitter enemies from conception, and the kings of frost and fire battled constantly for control of the world. And when fire and ice met, Mistgard sat and defended its shores. The united forces of Sprign and the Under-King, Fell, easily repelled the unorganized and divided armies of King Sumyr and Lord Wintyr.

But time, even for one as powerful as Sprign, crept slowly upon her. After many millennia, Sprign walked throughout the world less and less. Her emerald hair turned to flaxen silver, and she seemed more content to dwell amongst her great forests, tending her hives of bees. Sprign fell into long lapses of deep sleep, and while Sprign slept, her brothers would exert their dominance upon the world. All giants had their time and place in the realms—it had been such since their creation—and though she was near immortal, Sprign's time had come to an end.

CHAPTER 2

A MOTHER'S FAREWELL

PRIGN WAS DRESSED in a simple gown of green and amber, and her hair, normally intricately braided, had been brushed smooth. Ribbons of silver were tied to a graceful set of horns that grew from her head, and her body lay quietly on a bed of fresh moss, pine needles, and soft grass. Upon her breast lay a small crystal of purple amethyst, a gift from her brother Fell.

Sprign was mother to not only the Pandyr but all the creatures of Mistgard. They, too, came to bid farewell to their beloved maker. Tokens of respect were piled around her cairn. Wreaths of wildflowers and clutches of berries adorned her memorial. Large herds of elkhorn gathered around and placed bouquets of fresh leaves upon the mound. Tiny blackbirds and gray gulls flocked above in slowly moving circles and, one by one, dropped a pinch of moss or a bit of seashell on her earthen bed. A massive, one-eyed jaegyr hound, followed by his growling pack, bullied his way forward, leaving joints of meat and bone from a fresh kill. All the beasts of Mistgard gave what they could to honor the departure of the Den Mother.

After the tributes from the children of forest and sky came the gifts from the children of hearth and hall, and their offerings varied in nature as much as the clans themselves did.

JADEBOW

From the northern clans of the Iceclaw, Jadebow, and Ironbeard were animal totems carved from perma-ice, bows of yew wrapped in icy blue frost-bloom, and pinecones filigreed in shiny silver.

From the great clans of the south, the Sunspear, Hammerheart, and Mistcloak, came golden-wrought shields, stone warhammers wrapped in wreaths of glowing fire blossoms, and supple blankets of mistreed cotton.

The offerings from the central clans, the Thundermaw and Darkcloud, were the most intricate and lavish. The skilled carpenters of the Thundermaw carved an ornate wooden apiary adorned with dozens of beautifully lacquered honeybees. The Darkcloud were undoubtedly the finest painters and tailors upon the island, and they gave to Sprign beautiful silk banners dyed in her colors: green, amber, and silver. On each banner was an embroidered triangle with a corner pointing up like a mountain.

The clansmen nodded at the skill and craftsmanship of the offerings, some with approval and some with jealousy.

After the clansmen had laid their tributes upon Sprign's cairn, they fell back and watched silently. No one, neither Pandyr nor beast, spoke or snarled. All eyes were upon an old, silver-bearded Pandyr. He was a tall, imposing figure dressed in blues and grays, and upon his head, a large set of sprawling horns jutted out from under his mane. Though ancient in years, he clutched not a walking cane but a long black spear. He was known by many names. Called the Gray Rider and the Horned Hunter by the northern clans, to the southern clans he was known as Storm Spear and the Grim Gray One. But his most common name was the Storm Speaker. He turned toward Sprign and placed a braided wreath of flowering honeypine needles on the mound. Gently laying a hand upon the altar, he gave a solemn farewell. After a moment, he turned his attention to an ancient stone obelisk and spoke with a voice that sounded like gentle rolling thunder.

"The children of Sprign have paid their last respects, Under-King. We thank you for allowing us to say our goodbyes. Your sister, our mother, will be greatly missed." The Storm Speaker bowed deeply and joined the rest of the gathered Pandyr.

With a rumbling, the silent obelisk and the smaller ones around it awoke. The stones uprooted from the earth and, on legs of living rock, surrounded Sprign's mound. They joined their misshapen limbs, formed a crude dome, and reverted back to quiet, unmoving granite. Sprign's mound, once open to the storming sky above, was completely encased by the stone.

Only one obelisk remained separate from the dome, and on its surface a massive face formed and spoke. The face was as impassive as the surface from which it was formed. The voice rumbled with a gravelly tone.

"With Sprign gone, so are my ties to this upper world." The brooding face looked toward the Storm Speaker. "Goodbye, Oldest of Cubs."

A slight smile crossed the Storm Speaker's face at the title the Under-King used. It was the same name that Sprign had been fond of calling him. His looks belied his actual age of nine hundred and ninety-nine years upon Mistgard.

"So you will return to the Under Realm?"

"Yes," the Under-King replied flatly.

"And what of your brothers and the war that they will bring upon Mistgard now that Sprign has passed?" said the Storm Speaker.

"My brothers care nothing for me, just as I care not for them. I wish nothing more than to be gone from this upper world. I wish to be back amongst the stone and the earth. This upper world is wretched, where brother wars upon brother, and clan against clan. You surface walkers learned nothing of what Sprign taught you. She has left you now. And so, too, shall I."

The Under-King's face receded back to the stone's inanimate surface, and the obelisk that had borne his visage spoke no more.

CHAPTER 3

A GHOST IN THE FOG

NDER BRUISED AND SULLEN storm clouds, the eight clans of
Mistgard huddled together for the first time in many hundreds of
years. The clansmen stood grim and silent, pelted by a storm of
burning ice and fire that grew stronger with each labored breath.
The Storm Speaker looked around the Circle in the Sky as the
Pandyr gathered their belongings, and he spoke.

"So is this indeed the twilight of our people?" he asked, looking to the
clan chieftains.

The Sunspear chieftain, Byorgn, snorted indignantly at the Storm
Speaker. He was a large Pandyr dressed in fine garments and polished chain
mail. The Sunspear was the richest clan in Mistgard, and they were an arrogant lot.

"The Den Mother is gone, old one. You heard what the rock king said:
We are on our own," sneered the chieftain.

"That is not entirely the case. Sprign is still with us in many ways. In fact,
I was visited by Sprign just this morning," said the Storm Speaker.

The Den Mother had passed nearly three days before.

The Sunspear chieftain rolled his eyes, but many of the Pandyr looked

intently at the Storm Speaker. They had heard his prophecies many times before. To some of the Pandyr, he was an oracle and a mystic. To others, he was an oddity, and they looked upon him with doubt. He was called the Storm Speaker because he had the peculiar habit of standing on the cliffs during violent storms and allowing great arcs of lightning to blast him from above—or, as he would call it, to "speak" with him. So his words did not come as a surprise to all.

"She came to me in the early morning's fog, but not as the benevolent mother you've known in your lifetimes. No, she appeared to me in the way I knew her when I was but a cub so many years ago. In my childhood, she was known as the Great Huntress. She was dressed not in cloth and leaves but

in lacquered wooden armor, with a war spear, not a walking staff, in hand. And she gives to us this message . . ."

"Sunspear, let us leave," said Byorgn. "Let this madman prattle away to the storm if he so chooses, but the Sunspear clan will not be a part—"

"Children, listen well," came a familiar voice. It was younger and more vibrant than any of the Pandyr had heard it in hundreds of years, but the voice was undeniably that of Sprign.

The Storm Speaker's eyes crackled with volcanic green energy, and lightning struck his upraised spear. Behind him, a giant female figure appeared upon the clouds when the lightning flashed and disappeared when the thunder rolled. His voice rang out even amidst the howling winds, and the ghostly voice of Sprign floated and weaved amongst the Storm Speaker's words.

"My children," said the Storm Speaker and Sprign, "I was ancient when even the Oldest of Cubs was a boy, far older than the very mountains we live upon. But even I am as mortal as any being on Mistgard. My spirit will not linger much longer in this realm, and with my passing, there will be an imbalance in our lands."

There was a pause as stormy winds screamed from the north and south.

"My brothers come to Mistgard."

The Storm Speaker thrust his spear south, and lightning flashed. "From the burning crags of Firehome, King Sumyr and his fire giants rise up and march." The Storm Speaker stabbed his spear to the north, and thunder answered. "From deep in Icegard, Lord Wintyr will rouse his frost giants and descend upon our misty island. Even now, the oceans surrounding our mountains freeze. And when the oceans freeze, the giants will come. There will be war. And then there will be no more."

The Storm Speaker lowered his spear, the fire gone from his eyes. He was clearly weary from the display. The clansmen spoke in hushed tones. Never before had they seen the power of the Storm Speaker so clearly. Those who were once doubters of his abilities were now believers.

"What sort of trickery is this?" said Byorgn. "The Sunspear clan will return to our lands, and we will defend them if need be. The rest of you can believe this madman's ghost stories, but I will not be party to this hermit's rantings."

From the Hammerheart clan emerged a red-maned Pandyr, Thoryn, wide in shoulder and stout in frame. He moved past the Sunspear with an impassive look. The Hammerheart and Sunspear chieftains had no love for each other, and it showed.

"There is not much we can do, Storm Speaker, other than return to our halls and prepare for the coming battle." Thoryn paused for a moment, considering his words. "Those who wish may follow the Hammerheart back to our homelands. We have supplies and arms enough for all those who would fight this threat."

Byorgn laughed at the offer and stared at the gathered clans haughtily. "You can all run away together, for all I care. The Sunspear will stand against the threat on our own. We need no help from your barbaric lot."

Thoryn growled and stormed toward Byorgn, but he was stopped abruptly by a long black spear haft. Byorgn glared back at Thoryn mockingly and was soon flanked by his clansmen.

The Storm Speaker quietly eyed the Sunspear chieftain for a moment, then turned his attention back to the other clansmen. "I ask the chieftains of the eight clans to come with me."

The chieftains of Mistgard, minus the Sunspear, joined the Storm Speaker at the base of Sprign's cairn. He looked to them, and his voice boomed. "Doom is surrounding our island as we speak. The united armies of Lord Wintyr and King Sumyr march upon us. No longer do they war upon each other. With Sprign gone and the Under-King locked in his Under Realm, they will put aside their fraternal hatred and focus upon our lands." Wind ripped through the clansmen, and fire and ice seemed to acknowledge the Storm Speaker's words. "There is but one choice, and one choice alone. Chieftains of Mistgard, we must unite our people once again. We must put aside our petty differences and join together, for only together do we stand a chance of surviving. We must unite our clans."

The chieftains listened to the words and looked at each other hesitantly. The Storm Speaker continued. "But we cannot fight this battle spread out amongst our various clan territories. We must find a defensible area that we can hold. We cannot do so under the storms of Wintyr; already his breath freezes us to the core, as well as the land around us. No, we must journey far away, to where even the storms of Lord Wintyr himself cannot reach us. We must take our clans and go through the clouds to the birthplace of Sprign, the Aesirmyr Peaks. Even Wintyr's wrath cannot reach this blessed area. There, far above the storms, we can make our stand."

CHAPTER 4

UNIT3D

"LEAVE OUR ANCESTRAL HOMES? Retreat?" said Thoryn. "The Hammerheart will not flee our homeland and leave it to be fouled by the footprints of giants. My kin have been slaying the dogs of Sumyr for thousands of years; we were weaned on the blood of giants. The Hammerheart will stay and fight!" Thoryn returned to the other Pandyr and spoke loudly against the storm. "Fellow chieftains, I ask you to join with the Hammerheart. Join us, and with our combined might we will give the invaders a warm Mistgard welcome!"

The Hammerheart clansmen roared approval, as did members of the other clans. Their cheers were soon to be silenced by the Storm Speaker as his voice boomed across the plateau.

"This is no skirmish party sent to steal elk from our coastal lands!" he said. "You will be standing against the combined might of the frost- and fire-giant nations! A thousand giants will be but the first wave to march upon Mistgard. If the Hammerheart, or any clan, choose to stand here and fight, then their cubs, their mothers, and their clan will die to the last!" As he spoke these words, the swirling storm clouds above roiled furiously. The Storm Speaker breathed deeply and shook his graying mane slowly. "Forgive me,

Thoryn. I shout at you, Chieftain, as if you were naught but a newborn cub. Your heart is equally as strong as the Hammerheart name."

The Storm Speaker bowed till his long black beard dusted the ground. Raising his head, he continued. "Your heart is in the right place; it is the coming battle that is not. We are not retreating, young chieftain. We are simply taking the battle from the giants' hands and choosing the location from which we wish to fight them. For us to achieve victory, the Hammerheart and all the clans of Mistgard must unite and seek the safety of the Aesirmyr. Above the clouds, above the storms, we may have a chance of survival. But standing toe to toe with the armies of Firehome and Icegard, under ash and frost . . ." The Storm Speaker sadly shook his head.

Thoryn went to his clansmen slowly, considering the words as one would taste bitter medicine. From his wide waistband hung a massive stone hammer. He rested his hairy fist upon the short handle and looked toward his clan. "When my great-grandfather Thorg was alive, he would tell me many stories of the Storm Speaker, saying that he was a crazy old hermit, as likely to summon lightning during a clear day as he was to calm a storm that was ravaging the clans the next."

It seemed as if the gathered clansmen had heard similar stories, for they all nodded and jested together.

"My great-grandfather also said that, hermit or not, the Storm Speaker was as reliable as the stars in the sky, and was the wisest of all the Pandyr." Thoryn cleared his throat and continued. "I have always listened to my great-grandfather's words, and now, though it rubs my fur the wrong way, I will listen to them again." Thoryn drew the old stone warhammer from his belt and raised it high into the air. "We will follow the Storm Speaker to the Aesirmyr, and our hammers will stand as one with all the clans. By the hammer of my great-grandfather, let the Hammerheart offer ourselves to this cause!" he roared through his red beard.

The Hammerheart clansmen raised their hammers and cheered in return.

"Now, who will stand with us?" said Thoryn as he looked to his fellow chieftains.

Thoryn's gaze fell over them one by one until his eyes locked on a tall, lean-limbed chieftain dressed neatly in green and gray. The tall one sat comfortably on a beautiful golden elkhorn. The two chieftains stared at each other for some time, and the silence was heavy. The tall Pandyr rode forward and dismounted, eyes never leaving Thoryn until the two stood chest to chest. The Hammerheart was shorter, but his frame was nearly double that of the other. The tall one nodded, and Thoryn laughed as the rider raised his weapon, a polished longbow of golden yew.

"Though we stand a bit taller, the riders of the Jadebow will join this circle," said Ullyr, chief of the Jadebow clan.

A few moments went by, and soon another chieftain stepped forward, followed by another. A black broadsword was raised by Tyr'og, and a clawed gauntlet by Ur'sog, chieftains of the seafaring Ironbeard and Iceclaw clans. The Mistcloak and Thundermaw chieftains, Ulf and Mog'aw, raised long knife and giant axe to the circle of weapons. The dour chieftain Modyr of the Darkcloud clan raised his two-handed war club, and then they waited. All eyes fell to the missing Byorgn of the Sunspear.

After much time, Byorgn moved amongst the other chieftains and made sure he had everyone's attention. He cleared his throat and raised his golden spear high.

"Pandyr, by the golden lance of the Sunspear clan—"

"Let all the clans of Mistgard be united!" roared Thoryn, eyeing the Sunspear chieftain.

The clansmen cheered furiously and, for a moment, drowned out the winds. The Storm Speaker's voice rose above the din. "Nay, chieftains, we are still incomplete. There is still one more clan that needs to join our circle."

"What is this you speak of?" said Thoryn. "The eight clans are one on this day. By oath and honor, we join together as we have not for a thousand years."

The Storm Speaker looked at the united clansmen and offered them a smile. Far in the distance stood the silhouette of the Aesirmyr Peaks. It was toward the peaks that he pointed his spear. "When we reach the base of the Aesirmyr, we will find them, somewhere between the earth and clouds. We will find the ninth clan."

The gathered clansmen fell silent in an instant, all but one. The Hammerheart chieftain sputtered out words as if he were choking on them.

"The ninth clan?" said Thoryn in astonishment.

"Aye, Hammerheart," said the Storm Speaker through a frost-flecked beard. "A clan much like yours. I have seen them with my own eyes. They are a clan of warriors who rival the Hammerheart in battle prowess, and their archers are able to hit a target at a thousand yards."

The Jadebow clansmen laughed, and their chieftain gave an arrogant retort. "A thousand, you say? I'll believe that when I see it, Storm Speaker," said Ullyr mockingly.

The Storm Speaker smiled, looking at the chieftain. "Well, you will get the opportunity soon. You all will, for on the morrow we will journey to meet them. Even united, our numbers are still too few, and we will need the strength of the ninth clan to join us in our fight. Only together may we stand a chance. We will talk more of this later."

Baffled by the Storm Speaker's words, the chieftains and their clansmen were left muttering into their beards.

"Return to your camps and gather what you need. We will meet back here at dawn." With that, the Storm Speaker looked to the burial mound of Sprign. "Your children have united, Den Mother."

The Storm Speaker turned and moved slowly toward a pair of young Pandyr waiting for him. The old Pandyr stumbled, holding on to his spear for balance.

"Storm Speaker!" exclaimed a large, white-maned youth, but he was stopped with a gesture of the old one's hand.

"Nay, Frostpaw, I am fine. The day has taken its toll upon these old bones, but I can walk on my own."

The Storm Speaker stood at his full height and walked freely once again, but this act did not fade the worry upon the young Pandyr's brow. His female companion, Ursara, returned shortly after, holding the reins of an immense gray war elk, Traveler, the Storm Speaker's mount.

"Father, at least ride for a short while. Traveler is concerned," she said. Clearly, her eyes spoke a different name.

The Storm Speaker smiled at Ursara. Her feelings for her young companion showed all too well. "Traveler . . . is concerned, you say?" he said warmly. "Well, then, let me ride with my worried friend and ease her concerns."

Together, the Storm Speaker and Traveler, Frostpaw, and Ursara returned to their hall, known as Thunder's Home by the clans. When the group was but a tiny silhouette in the distance, the features of the Under-King, Fell, appeared once again on the giant obelisk to watch the Pandyr disappear. The face, composed of stone, seemed softer. Seconds later, it was covered with snow.

CHAPTER 5
PREPARING FOR WAR

THE REST OF THE DAY was spent gathering the herds of the Storm Speaker and preparing them for the pilgrimage. The war elk of Mistgard arrived in pairs or in large families, and they ran the spectrum in size, ranging from hulking stags to lithe fawns and does. The Storm Speaker sat on his wooden throne, where he communed with all the beasts of Mistgard. A small black bird named Gloam monitored the southern clans, while an enormous white albatross named Fog soared above the northern clans. Another name for the Storm Speaker was the One-Eyed Watcher, for when he sat on his throne, closed his eyes, and then opened one, he could see through the eyes of his animal companions: his left eye for Gloam, his right eye for Fog.

The Storm Speaker surveyed the clans from his hall, and the hours of daylight burned away into the dark of night. All through the cold evening's preparations, the snow continued to fall relentlessly. In the light of dawn, everything was coated in a bleak mantle of hoary frost. Soaring in the stormy skies were black Gloam and white Fog. Both bird and Storm Speaker watched the clans from amongst the clouds.

"The clans are ready, and they journey back to the Circle in the Sky," said the Storm Speaker as he stood and stretched his back. He grabbed his black spear and shrugged off the stiffness incurred from his night-long vigil. He looked around one last time and walked out of the tall double doors of Thunder's Home.

Ursara rode up on a black elkhorn named Cinder. Traveler was at her side. "The herds are ready, Father," she said. "They have been saddled and are eager to help bear the old and young up the Aesirmyr."

He nodded in approval. "Frostpaw, are we ready?"

"Yes, Storm Speaker. I have bolted shut Thunder's Home as best as I could. Though I fear it will do little to keep out an army of giants."

There was a look of profound grief in Frostpaw's eyes, and the Storm Speaker gave him a fatherly pat on his head. Thunder's Home was the only home the boy had ever known since the Storm Speaker had adopted him some twenty years ago, and though Frostpaw was not his child by blood, the Storm Speaker was immensely fond of the lad. Unfortunately, most of the clansmen felt differently, and this saddened the Storm Speaker greatly.

All his life, Frostpaw had been different. He stood hands taller than most full-grown Pandyr, and he was but a youth. His frame, still that of a young man, was already corded with muscle. But that was not the most remarkable thing about Frostpaw; rather, it was his coloring. The majority of the Pandyr bore thick coats of black and white fur and black manes. The southern clans, especially the Hammerheart, tended toward reddish brown in place of the black markings. Of the northern clans, the Jadebow had a sandy blond hint to their darker patches. Frostpaw's coat, on the other hand, was void of color. Frostpaw had a white mane upon his head that he wore long and free-flowing. And the fur that covered his muscular frame and arms was completely white. In some places, the white took on a bluish hue that made him look ghostlike. Instead of green, gray, or brown, his eyes were an icy blue.

The majority of the clansmen had never seen this type of coloring before. But many of the older Pandyr remembered it well. The coloring and those possessing it were called Wintyr-Born, and the birth of a Wintyr-Born signi-fied the start of a time of great strife for the clans. It always seemed to happen during the coldest months of Lord Wintyr's reign.

No one, not even the Storm Speaker, could predict when a cub like this would be born. It was said that cubs bearing these markings were uncontrol-lable and wild, filled with anger and rage; hence they were given the name Wintyr-Born, for the cubs were believed to embody the spirit of the lord of

Icegard himself. The Storm Speaker took great care in teaching the youth how to control his wild rages through meditation and calming the mind.

He has grown much since he joined our family so many years ago, thought the Storm Speaker. His gaze drifted from his adopted son to his blood daughter, Ursara. *Though they are not of the same blood, they used to fight as bitterly as any real siblings would . . . How much they have grown.*

One would never know that Ursara once had feelings of rivalry and jealousy toward Frostpaw over her father's attention, for over the years those feelings had changed into something of a different sort. Though she was several years older than Frostpaw, she was still very young by Pandyr standards, and she was already developing into a strong woman.

Ursara's demeanor had changed, and so had Frostpaw's. At one time, the youth would spend his free hours running with the bounding elkhorn herds, keeping as far away from the stern Ursara as he could. Now, the Storm Speaker saw the lad constantly at her side, and he even saw the looks they gave each other when they thought the One-Eyed Watcher wasn't watching.

"Come on, you two. We must be off now." He coaxed Traveler to leave. The gray elkhorn went reluctantly.

The three Pandyr left Thunder's Home, followed by the herds of elkhorn. Frostpaw cast one more look back at the lodge he called home, and without another word, he turned and walked with the herds to the Circle in the Sky.

He would never see Thunder's Home again.

CHAPTER 6
A FINAL GIFT

HE CLANS GATHERED AT the Circle in the Sky, and though it was now past dawn, the storm-clouded sky was still black as night, lit only by the terrible red glow from far-off Firehome. The Pandyr's coats and cloaks did little to warm them. Ember and ice fell as one, while the eight clans of Mistgard bowed and said goodbye to their fallen chieftains and elders who, like the Den Mother, were buried at the Circle in the Sky. Though the Pandyr were not a religious race, they did possess a deep sense of ancestral reverence.

Having no clan of their own, Frostpaw, Ursara, and the Storm Speaker walked to Sprign's mound, where they were greeted by the strangest of sights. The dome that once covered it was gone. The Storm Speaker smiled as Frostpaw and Ursara looked on in wonder. Soon, clan by clan, the Pandyr all gathered at the cairn, and they, too, marveled in awe.

Though the wind ripped at the Pandyr and the air was heavy with ice and sparks, it was eerily calm. The ground was free of snow and ash, and surrounding the burial mound was a large beehive. Around the hive droned green, silver, and amber honeybees. The apiary was crammed with honeycombs.

The Storm Speaker moved forward to the buzzing hive. The normally aggressive bees seemed strangely unperturbed at his approach. From the honey-fattened hive, amber-, green-, and silver-hued combs could be seen jutting out. The Storm Speaker reached slowly into the hive, pulled out a finger full of honey, and held it to his nose. "An odd smell for honey," he said quizzically.

Thoryn boldly strode forward and took a handful to his nose. With a snort, he bellowed, "It smells of fire blossom to my nose! The Hammerheart brought wreaths of it up yesterday to rest here on Sprign's cairn." Thoryn's chest swelled with pride.

Ullyr of the Jadebow came forward. He, too, took some of the strange honeycomb and waved it under his nose. "Bah, your senses are as dull as your hammer, red beard. Clearly it smells of the frostbloom brought by my clan just yesterday as tribute to the Den Mother."

A look of understanding crossed over the Storm Speaker's bearded face. He, too, knew the odd aroma the honeycomb conjured to his senses. "I think you are both correct."

The chieftains looked at the Storm Speaker.

"I do not mean disrespect, Storm Speaker, but I clearly smell frostbloom," said Ullyr.

The gathered Pandyr nodded, including Thoryn. The Jadebow were great trackers and had the keenest senses of any amongst the clans, and Ullyr was the best tracker of the Jadebow. It was said that the chieftain could track the shadow of an owl on a moonless night. Still, the Storm Speaker shook his head.

"This is not something that has a right or wrong answer, Ullyr. This is not something that the waking senses can trace. To my nose, it smells only of honeypine blossoms, the same tribute I left for Sprign upon her cairn."

The Pandyr gathered around, smelling the honey, searching for any hint of the phenomenon.

"By Sprign, what magic is this, Storm Speaker?" said Thoryn.

"By Sprign indeed," said the Storm Speaker, gazing at the cairn in thanks. He placed a bit of comb into his mouth and began to chew, slowly at first and then with more relish. A wave of warmth washed over him like a blanket that sat near the hearth. "It warms my bones like the strongest of mead, and it fills my belly with but a bite," he said. He let out a small belch and laughed. "It seems the tributes have been taken to heart."

The Storm Speaker started breaking off large bricks of honeycomb, motioning the chieftains to come forward. "Quickly, grab what you can and disperse it amongst the clans," the Storm Speaker said hurriedly, and he watched the commotion till the mound was bare of honeycombs. The bees and hive faded and were replaced by the lacquered wooden sculptures that they had been the day before.

The Storm Speaker looked at the gathered clans and motioned the elkhorn to move forward. "The herds of Mistgard have offered their help. They are half our number, so let only those in need ride upon our friends."

The clansmen scurried, taking large helpings of the tribute honey from their chieftains and then assisting the older Pandyr and mothers with young onto the powerful elk. Ullyr and the Jadebow, who had arrived on their own mounts, watched as the other Pandyr clumsily mounted the elkhorn. The Jadebow were born upon the saddle, while most of the Pandyr weren't accomplished riders.

The clansmen were quite thankful for the help provided by the Storm Speaker and Ursara. The same could not be said for those being helped by the young Frostpaw.

Frostpaw hoisted a worried-looking young Sunspear mother and cub and placed them both upon a heavy brown elk. There was a hard cracking sound, and Frostpaw was sent sprawling into the snow by the end of a thick oak spear haft. Atop a bleating elkhorn sat Byorgn, chieftain of the Sunspear clan. He was armored in the finest gilded chain mail and held a shield of polished steel that was shaped like a blazing sun.

"Be gone from my grandcub, Wintyr-Born, lest you bring your mark down upon him as well!" Byorgn bellowed.

A rumbling sound like an avalanche grew in Frostpaw's chest. He rose to his full height, and he glowered down upon the Sunspear chieftain. A volcanic blue fire blurred his vision. In his mind's eye, Frostpaw could see the Sunspear chieftain twisted and lifeless in his grip, eyes bulged and crossed in death.

Kill . . . kill in the name of your master! Kill for me, whispered a malevolent voice in his mind. Frostpaw ignored the words, closed his eyes, and breathed slowly. The violent blue murder that clouded his mind finally dulled, and the thunder eased in his chest. He felt a calm wash over him as the hand of the Storm Speaker fell upon his shoulder, patting him gently.

"Frostpaw, let us go see if there are others who need our help," said the Storm Speaker calmly, though the rage in his eyes never left the Sunspear chieftain.

Byorgn felt the Storm Speaker's fiery stare bore into him. After a moment, he grabbed the reins of the elk and left with his kin, returning to his clan.

Frostpaw and the Storm Speaker moved slowly back toward the staring clansmen. No words passed between the two, as both had dealt with this before. As they walked, the Storm Speaker mused over the exchange with grim satisfaction. Frostpaw had managed to control his anger perfectly.

Had this happened when I first found the lad, Frostpaw and the chieftain would both be bloodied . . . or worse. The rage that had once held Frostpaw captive as a youth now appeared to be locked away.

They walked back together to Ursara, who was smiling. She, too, had seen how Frostpaw had mastered the rage within him, but she mused to herself that it would have been nice to see the pompous Byorgn knocked off his mount and into the wet snow.

The Storm Speaker rode upon Traveler, and Ursara was on her black stag, Cinder. Only Frostpaw remained on foot, being too large for the elk to bear for any distance. The Storm Speaker looked at the lad fondly. *He has always preferred to run with the herds instead of being their burden.*

With a raised spear, the Storm Speaker drew the attention of the clans. "It is with a happy but somber heart that I address you. Why, only in this direst of times, have we joined together? The problems and conflicts that yesterday would pit clan against clan have not blown away with the storm. Perhaps after the hardships that have brought us here today are gone, we may continue our union, but it falls to each of you."

The Storm Speaker focused his gaze on Byorgn and let the moment hang. The Sunspear chieftain returned the gaze with a steely look and a snort. The Storm Speaker moved his attention back to the clansmen. "The only thing that matters now is the very survival of our people. Brothers and sisters, elders and cubs, our traveling will be slow and treacherous, but if we stay, our deaths will be immediate. Clans, we must leave."

"Hold," boomed a gravel-crusted voice.

CHAPTER 7

A SAFE HAVEN

THE CROWDS LOOKED TOWARD the singular obelisk that stood before them. From the rocky surface, the face of the Under-King appeared. The obelisk shook, and the column transformed into torso, arms, and legs. What was once silent stone was now the living form of the Under-King, Fell. He quietly gazed down upon the stunned faces of the Pandyr. He was a colossal figure to behold, massive in frame and form. He towered above the gathered clansmen as an oak did an acorn. Runes that had been carved on the moss-covered stone were now adorning his chest and arms like necklace and armband. Shards of quartz hung beard-like over his lichen-caked torso, glinting dully in the cold dawn air.

The Storm Speaker looked up at the Under-King as he walked over to the burial mound. The usually grim Fell appeared to be laughing quietly to himself, and the crystalline tinkle of quartz floated behind the sound of gravel as he spoke. "It appears my sister's spirit still protects her little cubs," said the Under-King.

The proud chieftains muttered and grumbled at the term cast at them, but they remained mostly silent. The Storm Speaker just smiled.

The Under-King smelled the honey and put a small jewel of the nectar in his mouth. For a moment, his rocky exterior seemed to warm, and the violet-hued quartz turned a rosy color. He looked at all the gathered clansmen, nodding solemnly. "I will aid your people, Oldest of Cubs, as Sprign would wish. She has provided you with food and warmth. I can provide you something else. I can provide your people a haven."

He clapped his hands together and slowly moved them apart, rock fingers curled and bent. The cliff shook, and its walls split open to reveal a great cavernous entrance. The Under-King beckoned the clans to enter.

"The war will be brutal to all," he said with a deep, resonating voice, "but the young will bear the burden the worst. Their bodies are not built for this. The warmth already leaves them. Children always suffer the most from war. If it pleases you, I will care for them while you make this war."

Strangled cries arose from mothers and fathers alike as they clung to their cubs. Clearly outraged, the burly Hammerheart chieftain stalked toward Fell. "While we make this war?" said the red-bearded Thoryn incredulously. "We did not ask for this war. It is your kind, you thrice-cursed giants, who bring this war to our home." His beard trembled as he ground his fangs together in anger.

The Under-King looked at the Hammerheart chieftain, his eyes boring into him, but Thoryn returned his gaze with a fiery countenance.

"My offer extends to you, too, little red cub." Fell continued, slow and measured. "And to all of the clans. You all may stay in my realm if you wish, safe from war, safe from the cold and the fire. In my realm, you would all be safe."

Thoryn's answer was immediate. "Ha! You mean hide in the face of battle? We will not be cowards, skulking in the ground like vermin while giants stomp and walk freely on the world above. I will protect Mistgard until my body lies on top of a pile of giants, if need be!" His hand gripped his hammer's haft, knuckles cracking with the force. The clans backed up the Hammerheart with applause and cheers.

The Under-King stared impassively at the throng. "And this is why those words were chosen. Little cubs, you and your clans could all be safe from war, safe from harm. Yet what makes you walk off proudly to the utter destruction of your kind? It is pride. Pride has killed more than any other weapon."

The Storm Speaker moved between the two figures, and his words parted the tension with the measured ease of one who was known to calm storms. "Is it not that same pride that our Den Mother, Sprign, showed to you when you offered her a place in your realm, Under-King? Is it not that same spirit that allowed her to live above the ground, to live free and to breathe air from open skies even though she was surrounded by the strife of your brothers, and was called upon to defeat them time and time again? It is the same pride that made Sprign what she was to all of us."

The Under-King solemnly looked down at the Storm Speaker. "You are right, Oldest of Cubs. It was indeed that pride and spirit that helped forge that being into the one we all loved. And it was that pride that led her to leave me—and to leave you—before her time."

Fell turned, walked toward the massive cave entrance, and spoke. "My offer still stands if you wish it," the Under-King said. The gathered mothers and fathers exchanged hesitant glances. "The young will be safe in my realm. No one, not even the combined might of my brothers and their armies, can enter without my approval. When your war is over, I will bring them back. To whatever is left."

The clansmen all stared in silence, and the Storm Speaker looked to the chieftains. "This is not a clan matter. This question needs to be answered by the parents alone."

Thoryn's bearing seemed to settle down a bit. "I'll not cower below the earth while I still draw breath, but to know that our cubs are safe will be a tremendous burden off our hearts."

Ulf, the sly chieftain of the Mistcloak clan, laughed. It seemed inappropriate as it pierced the moment's gloom. "Listen well, everyone, for I believe that is the closest thing to an apology that we will ever hear out of old Hammerheart. This truly is a momentous day."

His words were greeted with scattered laughter. He cuffed Thoryn on the back, and the burly Hammerheart chief brushed it aside with a scowl and, eventually, a laugh. "And I feel sorry for the Under-King's riches if he is watching over even one of those scurrilous Mistcloak cubs of yours. By the end of the day, he'll be the poorest king around!"

It seemed all of the clansmen were of one mind. Knowing that their cubs would be safe from harm would greatly help them face the coming storm. The clans decided to leave their young in the protective realm of the Under-King. Fathers and mothers said their goodbyes to daughters and sons. Great-great-grandcubs were given one last nuzzling by great-great-grandparents, and the passing moments were filled with grief.

When the children had been kissed and held, they moved into the cave and waved their goodbyes— all but one. A lone cub still stood outside the entrance, refusing to move. It was the daughter of the Hammerheart chieftain, little Thorgrid, and she was determined to have her way. She stood in front of her father, arms crossed in defiance.

"No, I will fight with the clans! I am a chieftain's daughter! I am Hammerheart!" she said adamantly.

Thoryn pulled his thick beard in frustration. "Come now! All of the others are being very well-behaved and are listening to their fathers."

"No," was all she said.

Thoryn's nostrils flared, and just as he was about to grab the girl by her red braids and hurl her into the cave like his mighty hammer, a white hand fell on his shoulder. It was Frostpaw.

"If it pleases you, Chieftain, I have a lot of experience dealing with headstrong cubs. Maybe I can talk to your daughter for a moment."

Before Thoryn could refuse, Frostpaw was off. He knelt down with his giant frame till he was eye to eye with the little Hammerheart, and he whispered and pointed toward the other cubs. From their worried faces, they must have heard what Frostpaw was saying.

Thorgrid's look of defiance turned into a smirk, then into an all-out, fang-filled smile. She ran back to her father and gave him a great big hug. "Don't worry about me, Father. I'll make you proud." Then she skipped over to her fellow clan cubs.

As the cave started closing, all of the clansmen waved or cried goodbyes. The children were also weeping and holding on to each other, saying farewell to their parents. The only one who didn't seem sad was young Thorgrid, who was waving to her father and smiling.

Fell stood stoically watching as the goodbyes were exchanged, and when all was silent, he spoke. "They will be safe with me," was all he said. He walked steadily into the mouth of the yawning cave, which closed with a sound of stone weaving into earth.

The Pandyr held each other, saying how this was the right choice. Still, it was little solace for the mothers and fathers. Soon they wiped the tears away and prepared to start their pilgrimage to the Aesirmyr. Only Thoryn stood perplexed. He walked up to the towering Frostpaw, his mind reeling.

"What in Sprign's name was it that you said to make that girl move like that? She is as stubborn as a jaegyr hound and harder headed than my hammer. What could you possibly have said to make her give up and willingly walk away from a fight . . . smiling?"

Frostpaw was taken aback, and he stared for a moment. Awkwardly, he answered the Hammerheart chieftain. "I, uh, all I said was . . ." Frostpaw stammered but soon found his tongue. "All I said was that with the parents gone, the cubs would be looking for someone strong and brave to lead them. I asked her if she knew anyone who could help out and take charge, to lead all the cubs till their parents got back."

Thoryn looked at the tall lad and then started nodding and laughing heartily. He clapped him hard on the shoulder and returned to his people. "Ha! Storm Speaker, you've got a gifted one there. The boy must be an alchemist, for he turned stubborn stone into pliable gold."

The gathered clansmen laughed, and the Storm Speaker let the moment continue for a little longer. He smiled at how Frostpaw blushed at the praise.

After the moment passed, the Storm Speaker addressed the clans. "Now, with the children safe, we can leave."

So the Pandyr, some on foot, others on elkhorn, departed the Circle in the Sky. As they passed the closed cavern that protected their cubs, they blew kisses and touched the wall gently. The eight clans of the Pandyr left their ancestral homes and started their journey to the far-off, mist-veiled spires of the Aesirmyr Peaks.

With the Pandyr gone, the Circle in the Sky was barren of life. Sprign's mound and a single obelisk sat silently alone under storm clouds, embers, and falling snow.

***

As the gray day turned to the first minutes of purple twilight, the cliffside trembled with cataclysmic force, and the earth split wide. The burial mound of Sprign shifted and slowly lowered into the open ground. Deep into the earth it went, until it was no longer visible. A large slab of rock crossed over the opening, sealing it from the outside world. All that was left was the monolithic obelisk that once bore the image of the Under-King. It did not stand as a grave marker. It stood as a watchtower.

A strange sound filled the air. Branches snapped, and the heavy thud of footfalls sounded in the Circle in the Sky, but they were not the tread of Pandyr or elkhorn. Large silhouettes emerged from the forests, and soon the Circle in the Sky was filled to capacity with a far different audience. An immense shape loomed in front of the obelisk, and the area that held Sprign's tomb just moments before began to smoke. Fire licked fiercely into the sky, but the ground seemed impervious to the blaze.

Soon, the crowds parted to reveal a truly colossal figure, and as it entered the Circle in the Sky, the fires went out and were replaced with a freezing coat of dark ice. But the stone beneath would still not be cracked. Fire and frost circled in the air, and though dwarfed by the gigantic figures, the obelisk spoke.

"Hello, my brothers."

It was all that was uttered before the obelisk was cleaved in two by a living sword of fire. An instant later, the obelisk was smashed and shattered by an axe of pure glacier ice. Howls rang out in the night, and the world trembled.

Upon the shores of Mistgard, giants walked.

CHAPTER 8

FIRE, BLOOD, AND ICE

UIDED BY THE SWIFT Traveler and the other elk, the eight clans of the Pandyr made their way through the dense forests of Mistgard. They traveled hard and had scant rest, and both Pandyr and elkhorn alike grew weary of the ferocious pace set by the Storm Speaker.

The warrior clans of Mistgard were used to direct attacks and rarely relied on evasive measures, with the exception of the Mistcloak clansmen. Since the first miles of travel, the cunning Mistcloak chieftain, Ulf, and his rangers had been busy setting traps and snares to alert the fleeing clans of any giant pursuers. The Mistcloak moved about the trees like wild hares, bounding and leaping through the dense undergrowth. Even Ullyr had difficulty marking the movement of the rangers of the Mistcloak clan.

Thoryn snorted and fumed. "Never in my fifty years have I run so fast and so far away from a fight!" His clansmen concurred with him.

"There will be war soon enough, Hammerheart. Look to the sky," said the Storm Speaker grimly. Through the lofty boughs of the ironbark pines, the Storm Speaker pointed toward the not-so-distant sky. The firmament was embroiled in the chaotic dance of beak, wing, and talon. Coastal gulls, led by the giant albatross Fog, flew in swiftly from the north. Squawks and caws filled the air. Ursara drew closer to Frostpaw, and he placed his large white hand upon hers.

"Look, Father," said Ursara fearfully.

"Indeed, my cub, our lookouts return. The armies of Wintyr raze the north." A swirling cloud of blackbirds came in from the south, led by the tiny Gloam. The small bird landed on the Storm Speaker's spear just as throaty roars boomed in the distance. "The armies of Firehome pillage as well. Look, the fires of Sumyr light the island!" the Storm Speaker said.

Smoky tendrils choked the sky, and cries rose up from the southern clans. "Our lands are under siege, Storm Speaker. We should be fighting, saving our homes! We run like scared cubs!" raged the Hammerheart chieftain. His clansmen echoed his sentiments. Hammers pounded on ironbark shields, and throats called for a return to their lands.

The Storm Speaker did his best to calm the clansmen. "No, we must push on to the Aesirmyr Peaks. There is nothing we can do under the fury of Wintyr." To mark the statement, a huge blast of icy wind ripped down from the clouds, felling oak and pine like tiny saplings.

"The fires you see are nothing but the burning of lodge, hut, and hall. If the Hammerheart or any of the clans had chosen to stand fast, then the fires we see now would be funeral pyres. We must choose to take the fight where we will have the advantage. Remember, we are united, and we will face this threat with all the might of the Pandyr. We must push on," said the Storm Speaker.

It took many of his clansmen to hold back the Hammerheart chieftain, but he knew the Storm Speaker spoke the truth.

The Pandyr continued up the mountain, and so, too, did the storms. The clansmen's pace was severely slowed by the relentless snow and ash. They traveled into the night, and the storms grew in strength and fury. The supply of honeycombs, dubbed "Wintyr's haven," was consumed at a tremendous rate in order for the Pandyr to avoid freezing to death. The old, even though they traveled on elkback, were feeling the effects of the murderous cold more than the others. The Pandyr journeyed through the mountainous terrain for days, and their flight was taking its toll on them all.

Finally, on a bitter, frostbitten afternoon, the eight clans broke free from the dense forests and entered a large, open expanse filled with frozen lakes and windswept plains. The clansmen stopped to rest and gazed upon the miles and miles of icy terrain. When the Storm Speaker spoke, his breath was thick with frost. "We enter the Tundyr," he said.

The clansmen walked upon the ice-packed earth with great eagerness. The Jadebow burst from the ranks of the Pandyr and rode hard across the frozen steppes, stretching the legs of their elkhorn and embracing the wide, open plains. The clansmen were all thankful for the change of terrain, and they surveyed the area.

"Ah, it feels good to be out from under branch and bough!" exclaimed the burly Iceclaw chieftain, Ur'sog. The Iceclaw and the Ironbeard clansmen were born mariners and seafarers. Tyr'og of the Ironbeard walked up and slapped the Iceclaw chieftain on his brawny back.

"Aye, it beats the cloying cages of oak and pine we've been trapped beneath for these many days. Look, these vast plains of grass seem like waves under the sky, just like the mother ocean," mused the Ironbeard chieftain. "We should have taught all these land walkers how to sail, and then we could have taken this war to Icegard and to the fiend Wintyr himself!"

The majestic spires of the Aesirmyr remained cloaked in black clouds of ash and ice. The clans rested briefly and then started toward the mountains, far across the plains. Behind the Pandyr, howls and thunderous roars could be heard in the forests. Bursts of flame and silvery sparks blasted from the snow-covered trees and illuminated the clouded skyline.

The Mistcloak clansmen laughed at the light show. "It seems as though something has found our gifts," said Ulf with grim satisfaction. "Unfortunately, we have little fire powder left, and the giants approach more quickly than I expected."

Ullyr rode up on his golden elkhorn, Dawnstrider, followed closely by his hunting pack of jaegyr hounds. A bark from the tall chieftain silenced the canines, and in the commanding voice of one who was used to shouting orders, he spoke. "On these open plains, the giants will be able to make better time. No trees or traps to hinder their speed. The Aesirmyr is only a few leagues ahead. Come, swiftly now!"

His words were drowned out by the peal of battle horns. Just south of their position, the chorus was accompanied by the cracking of oak and pine. Massive shapes crashed through the forest, and more than fourscore brutish figures of ice and fire charged across the frozen plain. The lapdogs of Icegard and Firehome were upon them, some hulking and misshapen, some supple and lithe. All roared and frothed with rage upon seeing the Pandyr. Their blue and red skin stood in bold contrast to the snow. Icy shards and obsidian rock protruded from areas where frosted and soot-covered armor was absent. All had a chaotic mix of tusks and horns jutting from their bestial maws. Amidst the blackened armor and furs of unknown origin, one thing was all too familiar to the horrified clansmen. Many of the giants wore old hides of torn black-and-white fur.

Though they were still a few hundred yards away, the eight clans could see that their enemies would be upon them soon. Like most of the younger Pandyr, Frostpaw had never seen a giant before, and he was taken aback at the size of the brutes. Each one stood heads taller than even Frostpaw's great height. "Storm Speaker, the giants attack," said the youth.

URSOG

The Storm Speaker marveled at how much he sounded like a little boy again. The elder Pandyr was about to give the call to arms when he was interrupted by a gusty laugh. The laugh came from the chieftain of the Hammerheart clan. Thoryn bellowed heartily, in good humor rather than in sarcasm. "No, lad, these little things are not giants. These gangly mongrels are giantkin. They are faster than normal giants and are as dumb as a bag of hammers."

The sudden appearance of their age-old enemies was exactly what the old warriors had been waiting for. A whirring sound cut through the air, and it was soon followed by another and another. The Storm Speaker did not need to look to know the sounds came from Thoryn and his Hammerheart clansmen. Each warrior whirled a giant stone warhammer, and as it arced through the air, each one created a distinct humming sound. It had been many years since he had heard the symphony of stone.

The Hammerheart chieftain yelled at the brutes with great zeal. "Welcome to Mistgard, you fatherless dogs!" He charged toward the giantkin and hurled his great weapon, causing the very air around it to crack like thunder. The hammer of Thoryn was soon followed by dozens and dozens more, and the chorus of thunderclaps followed. The weapons screamed across the plains and smashed into the rampaging giantkin. Stone hammers met frigid ice, basalt, and bone. The hammers of Thoryn and his clansmen returned to their hands frosted in ice or coated in slag. "Ha! We throw like little cubs. Look, we missed one!" Thoryn laughed.

Of the giantkin, only one remained. His fallen brethren lay decimated at his feet. Seeing the bent and broken bodies of his kin strewn about him, he turned toward the safety of the forest, blowing his battle horn. His escape and the wailing horn were stopped dead by a shaft of green oak that seemed to magically sprout from his back.

"That was a mere scouting party," said Ullyr, lowering his great bow. "With all the damned horn blowing and hammer whirling, the entire army will know our location. We should head full speed toward the Aesirmyr with no more delays."

The giantkin crawled to a kneeling position and strained to raise his horn, intent on letting out one last blast. Ullyr swiftly loosed another arrow. It smashed into the giantkin a moment before the trumpeter was impaled by another arrow—or, more precisely, by what looked like a feathered spear shaft. The arrow pinned the giantkin to the ground with tremendous force and left him a crumbled mess. The clansmen turned, weapons at the ready, fearing that they might be flanked.

Ullyr gazed in the direction the arrow had come from. Others followed his stare. The eagle-eyes of Ullyr as well as the wave-roaming eyes of Tyr'og and Ur'sog saw a group riding swiftly upon them. The trio rubbed their eyes, squinted, and shook their heads as if they were having trouble seeing something or, more likely, believing what they saw. Soon, others saw the strange shapes coming toward them as well.

Frostpaw looked on in disbelief. The Storm Speaker rested his hand on the boy's shoulder and spoke softly. "Come, Frostpaw, it is time that you should meet with them."

Frostpaw stared at the Storm Speaker for a moment and then looked back at the approaching group. The Storm Speaker, Frostpaw, and Ursara rode off toward the figures. The rest of the Pandyr seemed unsure how to proceed. The chieftains were wary, but they mounted their elkhorn and followed the Storm Speaker and his cubs.

Ullyr and the Jadebow were the last to leave. They stood marveling at the giant arrow that protruded from the fallen giantkin's back. Ullyr pulled the arrow out of the body and looked at it, impressed. "I must meet the bowman who fired this arrow," he said in awe.

With that, the Jadebow galloped off toward the approaching riders.

BEARZYRK

CHAPTER 9

THE NINTH CLAN

A S THE PANDYR NEARED the figures, their fear of giants was replaced with a different fear. The tension was immense, and they felt they would rather face a hundred screaming fiends of Icegard than what approached them at this moment.

The Storm Speaker stopped and raised his spear high. The largest of the newcomers also raised his spear. The two eyed each other. The Storm Speaker remained seated while the other dismounted a giant horned beast and stood next to it. Even upon Traveler, the Storm Speaker was dwarfed by the hulking figure. They spoke for some time, and though the clansmen could not hear what was being said, the demeanors of the Storm Speaker and the tall figure were not those of strangers talking but of old friends catching up on life. The stranger even gave a pat to Traveler, who also seemed unafraid.

Frostpaw stared in amazement, for what he saw in front of him he had only seen reflected back at him when gazing into a pool of water. Frostpaw slowly walked over to the Storm Speaker. Ursara was still at his side, but he did not seem to notice.

The strangers stood taller than the youth and were more heavily muscled. Their fur was long and braided, and they wore little more than cloaks and breeches. Thick beards fell from their jaws, and shaggy manes hung loose in

51

the frosty air. Though greater in bulk and stature, they looked like any other Pandyr from far off. As the figures came closer, one clear difference could be seen. They did not bear the black coloration of most Pandyr or the dark umber shades of the southern clans. Even the tawny Jadebow clan markings seemed dark compared to the strangers' coloring. The entire group, twenty strong, boasted coats of mottled gray and white, and all twenty bore the "mark."

All twenty were Wintyr-Born.

Their leader slowly approached the youth. He was huge, a good foot taller and wider than Frostpaw. He looked the boy up and down with the same icy blue eyes as Frostpaw's, though his were somewhat clouded with age. "Come, walk with me," he said with a snort. He turned and motioned for the boy to follow him. Frostpaw looked to the Storm Speaker hesitantly.

"I will be right behind you, son. You have nothing to fear," the Storm Speaker said warmly. "We are welcome here."

Frostpaw looked to Ursara, smiled softly, and followed after the leader. The other Pandyr looked on in stunned silence, and the Storm Speaker watched them calmly. "Chieftains, brothers, and sisters, I have met with a very old friend, and we have been offered food and shelter. We've only a few miles to go, and then we may rest," he said.

There was confusion amongst the clansmen, and words flew. The chieftains all spoke and then gathered around the Storm Speaker. "What in the— where are you taking us?" said Byorgn, chieftain of the Sunspear, through a flecked and frost-grimed beard. "We're to ride with these beasts? You brought us here, to them?"

The Storm Speaker sat high on Traveler and stared down at the Sunspear chieftain. He spoke loud enough for all the clans to hear. "I have done exactly as I said I would do, Sunspear. Today is a great day for all of Mistgard. For today we have claimed our first victory over the giant kings' armies, and we have been reunited with our long-lost family."

"Family . . . ?" Byorgn boiled with rage. "What madness do you speak of? They are Wintyr-Born, a whole cursed clan of them!" roared the chieftain.

The Storm Speaker started following Frostpaw and shouted back. "Indeed, they are a clan, Sunspear. Tonight we will rest by the fires of my old friend Frostvang, elder clansman of the Bearzyrk."

"The Bearzyrk?" said Byorgn apprehensively.

"Yes, the Bearzyrk," said the Storm Speaker. "The ninth clan of Mistgard."

CHAPTER 10

FATHER TO SON

THE STORM SPEAKER RODE a few yards behind Frostpaw and the Bearzyrk, while the other eight clans of Mistgard plodded slowly behind him. The storm picked up in intensity and ripped their cloaks about them. The cold was taking its toll on the weary clansmen.

We must reach the Aesirmyr Peaks soon, thought the Storm Speaker. *We are down to the last bits of honeycomb, and we don't have enough for everyone as it is. We must join with the Bearzyrk. It is the only way for the clans, the Bearzyrk included, to survive the coming war.*

Through the hail and snow, the Storm Speaker could see Frostpaw walking next to the hulking Frostvang. Frostpaw towered over his fellow Pandyr, but not so with the Bearzyrk. It appeared that neither talked. They simply walked side by side, seemingly oblivious to the storm.

He almost looks small again . . . so much like when I first found him, thought the Storm Speaker.

***

It was nearly twenty years ago when the Storm Speaker first discovered the young Frostpaw. He was sitting on his throne, monitoring the daily routines on the island, when Gloam, the black bird, picked up a strange sight. The Storm Speaker closed his eyes for a moment and slowly opened his left eye. It was as black as coal and sparkled in the hearth's glow. It was through Gloam's vision then that the Storm Speaker watched.

Monitoring from above the trees, the Storm Speaker saw a young Pandyr, a cub no more than five years old, running swiftly through the forest. He darted in and out of the trees and appeared to follow a herd of elkhorn. He was not chasing them as a predator; he was running as one of them. He moved with the fleet herd, leaping and dodging boulder and oak alike. His young frame was naked with the exception of a ragged cloth he wore around his waist.

The sight of a lone cub lost in the wild was more than enough to awaken the Storm Speaker from his mystical visions, but there was also a darker message. The feral youth bore a ghostly white coat, and on his head was a matted shock of white hair flowing freely. He bore the mark of the Wintyr-Born. The Storm Speaker sat for a moment. *There has not been a Wintyr-Born in many hundreds of years. If what the legends say is true, then grim times are approaching.*

He leapt from his throne and ran outside the doors of Thunder's Home. The Storm Speaker made a series of high-pitched screeches, and soon a large shadow fell over him. Moments later the great wings of the albatross, Fog, bore him swiftly toward Gloam. Through the treetops they soared until they found the strange youth, and an already surprising sight became even more extraordinary.

The youth stood surrounded by a pack of ravenous jaegyr hounds. He was on his own with the exception of an old brown elk and a small gray doe. The latter was clutched in the boy's left arm, her leg bloodied from the fangs of one of the hounds. In his other hand was a large icicle. The hounds circled the youth, trying desperately to get at the old elk he defended. The youth roared at the hounds, foam flying from his maw, eyes blazing blue.

Suddenly the youth, doe and ice blade in hand, charged into the jaegyr hounds, more beast than boy. Though just a small lad, he was surprisingly strong, and he managed to wound many of the hounds. The boy slashed and stabbed at them, leaving many to a final sleep. Had the times been less drastic, the pack would have scattered, preferring to find prey with less fight to it. But times were desperate, and food was scarce during Wintyr's reign. The hounds tore back at the boy, and soon both hound and hunted were bloodied. Though the boy wounded and killed several hounds, many still were left, and the pack stood staring at him. The hounds' blood-red eyes bore into eyes of blue fire, neither side willing to quit.

The smell of blood was heavy in the morning air, and the hounds, ribs visible against their sides, came up with an alternative idea. They turned their attention away from the boy and tore hungrily into their fallen pack members. Fights ensued among the ravenous canines as they snapped and bit at one another. The carcasses were dragged across the ground, leaving dark, steaming rivers in the muddied snow. The leader of the pack, an old brindled brute with a shaggy-maned nape, looked back at his enemy through a scarred face that, thanks to the boy, was now missing an eye.

The Storm Speaker silently laughed. *This will be a bitter feast for ol' Fenryr and his dogs,* he thought with grim satisfaction. Fenryr and his pack of hounds had been the scourge of the elkhorn herds for years. It seemed the old dog picked the wrong fight today.

Sensing something in the trees, Fenryr let loose a howl. The beasts, beaten and battered, turned and disappeared into the forest.

The boy fell to the ground. Hound blood mixed with his own to stain his white coat an odd pink hue. Though some of his wounds seemed deep and painful, they appeared not to bother him in the slightest. Unconcerned for himself, he looked to the gray doe and tore off a shred of his loincloth. He grabbed a handful of snow and cleaned the doe's wound as best he could.

If he'd let the pack have the elk, he could've escaped unharmed, thought the Storm Speaker. *He fought for them as he would for his own brother and sister.*

The old elk stood slowly, favoring a twisted hoof. He sniffed the air and looked in the direction where the Storm Speaker remained hidden from sight. The elkhorn bolted through the trees, eager to find the herd.

The Storm Speaker watched as the lad tended to the wounds of the small doe. As soon as the boy was done, the Storm Speaker walked out and spoke gently. "The laws of the forest do not apply to you, do they, young one?" he said. "Where the old should fall, you would help them up. Where the lame would be prey, you would be their protector. Such a heart does not belong in the forests of Mistgard. While noble in gesture, it can hurt the balance of the wilds. A caring heart like yours is not meant for the world of beasts."

The Storm Speaker approached the boy slowly. The boy stared at him in wonder and, without a hint of fear, walked up to him. The gray doe limped slightly. The youth picked her up and held her close. Then he looked at the

giant Storm Speaker and touched the old one's arm. Taking the Storm Speaker's hand, the youth placed his tiny paw in the center of it. He gazed at the face of the wise old Pandyr, gripped his long beard, and then rubbed his own chin.

The Storm Speaker laughed. "All in good time, little one. Are you hungry? Do you want food?" He gestured as if he were eating with a fork. The Storm Speaker erupted again with laughter at the boy's strange expression. "Come. Better to let you smell what I am talking about than watch me act like a fool." He held out his hand to the young one. "Come." He beckoned. "Let's go tend to those wounds of yours, shall we?"

The Storm Speaker turned to leave but noticed that he walked alone. Looking back, he saw the lad standing there, holding the gray doe in his arms. The Storm Speaker nodded. "Ah, I see. Yes, yes, by all means, bring your friend. We will tend to her wounds as well."

He removed his cloak and swung it around both cub and doe. The boy rubbed the thick material while the doe tried vainly to free her head. The boy looked up at the Storm Speaker with exhaustion and snuggled into the coarse linen cloak as if it were of the finest Darkcloud silk.

"Warm, isn't it?" The Storm Speaker smiled. "My daughter made it. Not only is she a fine tailor, but she can cook the most wonderful potato stew, spicy enough to boil your blood. She's a few years older than you, but I think you'll like her enough. But I warn you: She is a stern little one."

The Storm Speaker laughed as he helped the cub—still holding fast to his companion—upon the giant bird. There was little time for the boy to realize what was happening before the fleet Fog lifted up into the air with a screech and the beating of great white wings.

CHAPTER 11

THE HALLS OF THE BEARZYRK

A FRIGID BLAST OF WIND AWOKE the Storm Speaker from his memories. The warm embrace of sleep had finally taken him away, but only for a moment. The gentle, measured rocking of Traveler did not help him stay alert. The Storm Speaker adjusted himself to a better position and patted the gray elkhorn beneath him, noting that Traveler's stride was as sure as ever. The scar she bore from the jaegyr hound bite was barely noticeable now beneath her coat. He touched her fondly, and she bleated out a few words that only the Storm Speaker and her herds would understand. He rode toward Frostpaw and the Bearzyrk Frostvang, who gave him a slight nod.

"It is good to see you awake, Dark Beard," rumbled the Bearzyrk. He seemed to be choosing his next words carefully. "Though, to tell my friend the truth, your beard is not as dark as I remember. Perhaps it is time for a new name for you." This was followed by a faint laugh. Though silver flecked with age, the Storm Speaker's beard and fur were still as black as pitch compared to the clansman of the Bearzyrk.

"I have more than enough trouble remembering all the names I already have. I believe I'll keep it as is," the Storm Speaker jested.

Frostpaw walked between the two in silence. Frostvang pointed at the mountains directly in front of them and spoke to the clans. "Here we are. We will enter between the two cliffs and journey inside the mountain."

Frostvang, the Storm Speaker, and Frostpaw silently proceeded forward. The Storm Speaker noticed that Frostvang was looking at the lad from time to time. The Bearzyrk glanced at the Storm Speaker and nodded. The Storm Speaker nodded as well. "Frostpaw, be a good lad and tell Ursara and the others we shall be stopping soon. Tell them for me, will you?"

"Yes, Storm Speaker," he said, and he strode back toward the others. When he was far enough away, the Storm Speaker looked at the old Bearzyrk.

"What do you think, Frostvang? Are my eyes finally failing me?"

"Nay, I see it too. There is blood shared between us, no doubt. The same shaped eyes, and that pure white coat!"

The Storm Speaker put a hand on the big bear's shoulder. "I'll leave it to you to tell him in your own time."

They went on in silent thought till they approached a large crag in the mountainside. The Storm Speaker was somewhat confused. "I never knew the Bearzyrk took permanent homes. I was always under the impression that the Bearzyrk was a nomadic clan."

"Most of the year we travel about as we please, roaming the Tundyr and the peaks, hunting, and taking trophies during the times of Sprign and Sumyr. During the time of Fell, we save up our meat and drink, and during Wintyr's time, we seek the shelter of our mountain dens. We Bearzyrk have only ourselves to rely on. Only the most stout and hearty of my Long Coats can weather this storm." Frostvang gestured proudly toward his fellow Bearzyrk following close behind him. "The rest are deep within the cliffside, lounging in the hot pools inside the belly of the mountain. This chill is the worst we have ever experienced . . ." The Bearzyrk looked inquisitively at his old friend.

"What is it?" said the Storm Speaker casually, but his eyes were alight.

"Meaning no offense, Dark Beard, but how is it that you and your gentler clansmen endure such an environment? It is cold upon the Tundyr and even colder during these end times. How is it that you and your clans ride about as if this were just a normal day?"

The Storm Speaker tossed a piece of the magic honeycomb to the Bearzyrk, who sniffed it and popped it into his mouth. His eyes showed his wonder, and he chewed it up swiftly and belched.

The Storm Speaker smiled wryly at the Bearzyrk. "And I would say the same to you, old friend. What did the Den Mother give to the mighty Frostvang and his Long Coats after their offerings were received?"

Shaking his head, Frostvang laughed, removed a large skin from his side, and tossed it to the Storm Speaker. "Mead," he said.

The Storm Speaker took a pull of the skin and nodded in approval.

Frostpaw ran up, his heavy feet crunching through the snow with ease. "They are ready, though Byorgn and his Sunspear are putting up quite a fuss. Nobody seems to care, though. They would rather sit with the Wintyr—the Bearzyrk—than freeze to death," said Frostpaw with a hint of bitterness in his voice.

The Storm Speaker handed the skin to the boy. "Then there will be no mead for those crying spears, so you can drink their share."

Frostpaw sniffed the skin and blinked as if trying to clear his head. Slowly, he tilted back and took a swig. He had a healthy pull, and the clear fur on his face seemed to redden from the flushed skin beneath it. He coughed, but the boy's eyes burned with approval.

As they continued on, the Storm Speaker told Frostvang about the past week's events, from the uniting of the clans and Sprign's magical honeycomb to the agreement made with the Under-King about the cubs. Frostvang, in turn, told of how the Bearzyrk had honored the passing of the Great Huntress (as they called Sprign) with a feast and tributes of mead, meat, and trophies of war, followed by the burning of a giant wattle-and-thatch effigy of the Huntress.

Though the Storm Speaker listened, his eyes did not fail to notice two lupine shapes that followed them. They were crafty enough not to let their presence be known even to the keen-eyed Jadebow, but there was nothing that could hide from the One-Eyed Watcher. Gloam and Fog soared over the slinking figures, darting and weaving, sending them scurrying, letting them know they had been seen. With a few futile growls, they fled. Ullyr's powerful jaegyr hounds gave chase only to be called back by a fierce bark from their golden-maned master. It was hardly needed, for the two lithe forms scampered quickly out of range of the stout jaegyr hounds, taunting them with yaps and yelps. The Storm Speaker watched them melt amongst the crags and disappear amidst the cliff rocks.

"Old Grymir still watches, eh?" mused the Storm Speaker.

"Always. As do you," retorted the Bearzyrk with a snort.

The Storm Speaker reached into his side bag and pulled out the last of his honeycomb. He handed it to the Bearzyrk. "Here, Frostvang, take this," said the Storm Speaker as he casually brushed away his friend's protestations. "It is only a few days' worth, but add it to your mead barrels. It should help take Wintyr's edge off of those who are—how did you suggest it? Less stout and hearty?"

They both laughed. The entrance was ahead, and the Pandyr followed the Storm Speaker and Frostvang into the heart of the mountain.

CHAPTER 12

WHEN BOW MEETS ARROW

HE PANDYR TRAVELED DEEP within the mountainside. The chasm walls jutted up out of the earth, protecting them from the full brunt of Wintyr's wrath. Still, the cold was relentless. Giant beasts were housed in crude stables, and the Pandyr were soon told that the Bearzyrk called these gargantuan animals spearhorn. They were a domesticated breed of the wild ones found wandering the great frozen lakes of the Tundyr. The Bearzyrk used many of them for personal mounts and labor. Their thick pelts also adorned the backs of the Bearzyrk, much to the disgust of Byorgn.

"Barbaric devils, the lot of them," he muttered. Many of the Pandyr felt the same as the Sunspear chieftain. The Pandyr's relationship with their herds was one of mutual giving, as opposed to that of master and servant. The herds provided milk and transportation to the Pandyr, and the Pandyr provided care, shelter, and protection.

Onward they traveled until they were standing in front of a large set of weathered, frost-covered doors. Frostvang motioned to his men, and they lumbered forward and opened the heavy doors. A great gust of hot air blasted onto the gathered Pandyr and turned to icy mist almost immediately. The inside of the mountain was ablaze with a welcome heat and humidity that they had not experienced in many days.

"Come in and warm your bones," Frostvang said to the Pandyr. "The elk and hounds can huddle amongst the spearhorn for warmth. It is actually quite warm there if they can tolerate the smell." He laughed and entered the cave.

The Pandyr moved into the hall, some in wonder and others in horror. The inside of the mountain was massive and easily housed the entire Bearzyrk clan. Furs littered the floor, and great fires raged. Vast pools of sulfurous water bubbled from the ground, and Bearzyrk sat and soaked in the wet steam. Huge tables were covered with roasted meats and horns of mead. The high walls were adorned with the heads of beasts, some the likes of which the Pandyr had never seen. The hall was filled with smoke and steam and smelled of sweat, cooking meat, and fermented drink. The Bearzyrk glared at the Pandyr clans with mistrust, but they fell back to their laden plates and frothing mugs when Frostvang's cloudy eyes bore into them.

The smell of charred flesh was difficult for some of the Pandyr to stomach. Their diet consisted of mountain vegetables and roots, berries, milk, bread, and honey. Some of the coastal and seafaring clans ate the eggs of gulls and albatrosses. The Pandyr were friend to all the animals of the forest and considered them to be almost kin. Never did they feast on the red flesh of animals, which the Bearzyrk did with relish. Fanged jaws tore into hunks of roasted beast, and bones were gnawed, snapped, and sucked for the marrow. Many Pandyr felt pangs of sickness roiling in their bellies and had to move to corners less occupied by the carnage. Even the Storm Speaker looked uneasy as Frostvang tore a leg off of what appeared to be a spearhorn calf that was spitted and cooking over a fire.

The Bearzyrk spoke to the old Pandyr between mouthfuls of meat and bone. "Please, eat and rest. If we are running short, we can spit another spearhorn, or one of your goats if you prefer that."

The Storm Speaker eyed the Pandyr, trying to quell some hostile looks. He turned to Frostpaw. "Frostvang and I are to meet with the Bearzyrk elders shortly and talk of the events that are upon us. Please rest and tend to the old and sick."

"Shall I go with you, Storm Speaker?" said Frostpaw, and the old one smiled. Despite all the day's events, the boy still concerned himself with filial obligations, though his eyes burned with questions.

"Nay, Frostpaw. You and Ursara go to the fires and warm your coats. And more important," he said, gesturing to the Bearzyrk, "talk with them."

The Storm Speaker and Frostvang disappeared down a long hallway and were soon out of sight.

The boy and Ursara went to the firepit in the center of the room. It was crowded with Bearzyrk, all drinking and eating, and they looked at the two with little interest. All of the Pandyr had made their way into the cave, but they still stuck close to their clans. Most tried to keep themselves away from the barbaric Bearzyrk. Ullyr had no such concerns. The meat and blood did not bother the Jadebow in the slightest. He and his clansmen were nomadic riders of the forest, and such sights were just part of the balance of the wild.

The Jadebow chieftain walked forward and stood upon the giant hearth, a massive arrow in his hand. He nearly had to shout to be heard over the din of the Bearzyrk. "Who here can shoot such an arrow as this and hit his mark? Who here makes such a shot that causes the Jadebow chieftain to gush like a newborn cub?"

The chieftain of the Jadebow was answered with silence. Clearly irked at being ignored, he leapt atop a table and raised the arrow high. Most of the Bearzyrk looked at him with indifference or disdain as he toppled over carafes of mead and plates of meat. A bull-like voice echoed in the chamber.

"Jadebow . . . Jadebow, you say?" Near one of the firepits stood a Bearzyrk of staggering proportions, easily as tall as he was wide. He lumbered over to the chieftain and looked him over. He wore a faded gray cloak that once might have been green before years in the sun had robbed it of its color. "Who are you, little one?" he said, tilting his head.

Ullyr looked perturbed by the condescending title given him by the Bearzyrk. He fired back at the big bear with all the bearing of a chieftain. "I am Ullyr, archer, rider, and chieftain of the Jadebow clan. How is it that you know of our name, ponderous one?" he said.

The Bearzyrk thought for a moment, and as if coming out of a haze, he answered. "I am Ullstag, archer and rider. And though I am no chieftain, I know of the name Jadebow, for I, too, am Jadebow."

CHAPTER 13
AMONG THE ELDERS

HE STORM SPEAKER AND Frostvang walked through a passage in the rear of the big hall and wandered down the corridor. The heat was overwhelming, and for a moment, the Storm Speaker almost longed for the frosty winds outside. The two entered a dimly lit chamber that Frostvang called the Den of the Elders. It was here that the Bearzyrk clan was governed and ruled.

It was a large room, not as large as the hall they had left earlier, but what it lacked in size it made up for in splendor. It was lined with exotic furs and coats of arms of ancient make. The elders, who were gathered around a reflecting pool on cushions of fur and cloth, motioned the Storm Speaker and Frostvang forward. By the look of it, Frostvang was but a cub compared to some who were near the bubbling pools. The steam was stifling, but the elders sat comfortably. After bowing to them, the giant Frostvang took his place amongst them and sat down without a sound.

Sitting on a large boulder at the center was the wisest of the Bearzyrk, Grymir, and behind him were his wolves. They approached the old bear and sat at his side. They eyed the Storm Speaker, who was directly opposite Grymir on the other side of the pool. There were no cushions or pillows for the Storm Speaker to sit on, so he remained standing.

69

"I'm listening, Storm Speaker," said the old Grymir. Though younger than the Storm Speaker by many hundred years, he looked far more ancient. His white coat was tied in various braids, and his fur was matted and painted with clan markings of the Bearzyrk. Life was bitter on the Tundyr, and it showed on Grymir's face. It was weathered and deeply lined, though his blue eyes were still keen and bright.

The Storm Speaker bowed. "And greetings to you too, Grymir, and to all the council. It is a pity we must meet in such dire circumstances. Your clan looks as strong as ever, a testament to the council's leadership." The Storm Speaker bowed again and continued. "The clans of Mistgard have united. In these times, we have all chosen to put aside our old feuds and hatreds. But we are still not complete. We have one more clan to meet with, to join together with. We—I have come to ask the Bearzyrk to join together with their lost brothers and sisters and stand with us against our common foe. Without the might of all the clans of Mistgard, we all shall fall to the wrath of the giants."

The old Bearzyrk laughed heavily. It was not a pleasant laugh of mirth but a dry and harsh one, lacking any humor and filled with contempt. "You wish the Bearzyrk to join the eight clans of the Pandyr? Now? After all these years? Don't be a fool, old one. You know better than any that our kinds do not belong together. You must remember that it was your people who cast the Bearzyrk out. It was your kind who banished us to the wilds, to live amongst the beasts when we were but cubs not even weaned from our mothers' milk. And now, with the twilight of Mistgard at hand, you come to us for unity, for brotherhood? If these be our last days, so be it. We will face them as we always have: on our own."

Grymir coughed a dry, jagged cough that shook his body. He leaned forward and breathed deeply of the steam, which seemed to soothe his spasms. "Now the Pandyr, the ones who banished us years and years ago, will know what it is like to be alone against the world," the old Bearzyrk mocked.

The Storm Speaker broke the Bearzyrk's scornful laugh. "Not all loathe your kind; not all fear. Who was it who brought the lost ones to your clan over these many hundred years? Who now raises one of the Bearzyrk as his own? Many of the Pandyr have grown up around one of your kind and—"

"And how has that been for the boy, Storm Speaker? Have the clans embraced the young one with a mother's arms? Have they welcomed him into their hearts and halls?"

The Bearzyrk's wrinkled face was twisted up into a smile, and after a pause, the Storm Speaker answered quietly. "He has had his share of problems, and he has weathered them as best as a boy can." The Storm Speaker looked intently at the council. Frostvang sat with his great head lowered. The old Pandyr continued. "He still seeks the clans' approval. Even after all these years, the boy still has hope that old fools will one day learn not to judge the present by the deeds of the past. He hopes that minds and hearts will learn to forgive."

The Storm Speaker bowed low and turned to go. "I thank the council for its time. I will inform the others that we will proceed on our own."

For the first time during the meeting, Frostvang spoke. "I have promised the Storm Speaker and his kin shelter for the night. Also, I would speak with the young one the Storm Speaker brought with him; he should know our history."

Grymir looked to his fellow councilmen and muttered something. After a few quick nods from the others, he addressed the Storm Speaker. "The council will allow the boy to stay if it pleases you, Storm Speaker."

The Storm Speaker merely nodded and turned to leave. Frostvang rose from his spot and followed the Storm Speaker down the hall. It was many moments before he spoke. "I am sorry, Dark Beard. We of the Bearzyrk know what these times bring. We know what we are facing. Yet the council is too old to change its ways. Come, let us join the others."

The Storm Speaker and Frostvang left the Den of the Elders in silence.

CHAPTER 14
THE LEGEND OF GHOSTMANE

ULLSTAG LOOKED AROUND at the throng of Pandyr and Bearzyrk. He took a long drink before speaking. "Many years ago—five hundred and ten, to be precise—I was brought here by the Dark Beard, or the Storm Speaker, as he is known to you Pandyr. Here I was greeted by others of my kind. At the time, I was the youngest of the Bearzyrk. But over the next few hundred years, more came. Some were cubs; some were like the boy here." Ullstag pointed at Frostpaw. "We, in turn, would raise them. To my memory, there has never been a female Bearzyrk, so we cannot breed amongst our kind. There were never any young about until the Dark Beard came with them. Ha! But when he delivered a new cub, you would see this group of giant-slayers and beast hunters turn into a bunch of fools, falling over themselves, wanting to help cub-sit the little ones."

The big bear smiled broadly, lost in the past. "We would raise them together. We would teach them how to hunt, how to ride, and how to build fires strong enough to burn in the bowels of Icegard itself!" A pall crossed over his face, and he suddenly looked very old. "But for some reason, the arrivals stopped, Byorgar being the last. I believe he died fighting giants in Icegard about fifty years ago. He was the youngest of our kind, at two hundred and some odd years."

"Died? In Icegard? Fighting giants?" said Thoryn, blurting out from a horn of mead he had snatched up. The brew was clearly having its way with the Hammerheart chieftain.

The old one furrowed his brow and tilted his head. Coming to a conclusion, he nodded apologetically. "Ah, I am sorry. You are correct, red one. It was little Hjolnr who died in Icegard. Byorgar died in Firehome."

Mead flew out from Thoryn in a huge spray. "Now you are battling in Firehome? I think the mead has gotten to your head, old one."

Ullstag laughed. "By the Great Huntress, no. I don't drink that swill. I brew up that fizz for the younger clansmen. They cannot stomach full mead like I can. If you like, come try a mug of this," he said as he lifted up his great drinking horn. "This will turn your coat white!"

"*Can't stomach?* Give me that. I'll drink this down to the bottom with naught but the suds left for you."

The mighty Thoryn downed the entire horn and tossed it back to Ullstag, who was somewhat impressed. He gave Thoryn a pat on his back.

"Someone fetch my personal barrel! We'll be needing another horn or two for my little friend and me," he said loudly.

Thoryn put up his hand and waved it. "I think that did it for me. It was a good brew but nothing that . . . It's rather hot in here, don't you think?" Thoryn crashed into the table face-first, upending it and sending the old Bearzyrk's bow flying.

Ullyr leapt as gracefully as an elkhorn and grabbed the weapon before it could hit the cave's floor. He marveled at the size and craftsmanship. It was a gigantic weapon, nine feet long and made out of what looked like carved horn. Etched into the bow were notches so numerous that it was scarred from end to end. Ullyr reverently handed it back to Ullstag. "What is it made of, old one?"

The Bearzyrk easily grasped the weapon and righted the table. He put the bow back in its familiar place. "It is made from the horns of my old friend Cliff Breaker. Of course, you know we Jadebow have an affinity for riding, and when I first arrived here, I was very lonely. I soon struck up a friendship with an old spearhorn, and over the years, we rode to battle together. We were the menace of both Icegard and Firehome. Alas, he died many years ago in Icegard. I brought back his body, and I made this bow from his horns. For years, I cut a notch in it for every kill we made together, but I have since stopped counting. Otherwise I would have whittled this bow in two!"

Ullyr thought of Dawnstrider and all the times they had fought and survived together. That seemed like nothing compared to the danger Ullstag had faced and now spoke of as casually as if he were telling cubs a bedtime story. "How long have the Bearzyrk been warring with the giants?"

The Bearzyrk shrugged his massive shoulders and pondered. "For as long as I remember, and for hundreds of years before that as well. The first of our kind, Ghostmane, took the entire Bearzyrk clan to the very hearts of Wintyr's and Sumyr's realms, even fighting the archfiends themselves!"

"Ghostmane?" It was the first time Frostpaw had spoken. "What happened to Ghostmane?"

Ullstag finished a sip of mead and answered the boy. "Ha! He battled for years and years. The older he grew, the bolder his raids. Our numbers were too small to mount a full war against the giants, but he had a plan. The first part was to go to Firehome and challenge the greatest of fire giants, King Sumyr. Ghostmane and Sumyr battled for days, and every weapon Ghostmane used against the Fire King turned into slag when it touched his molten skin. Exhausted, Ghostmane fell to his knees, defeated. The Fire King gloated and jeered at Ghostmane, but when Sumyr was going to deliver the killing blow with his giant black sword, the old Bearzyrk made his move."

The crowd was silent as Ullstag let the moment grow. Finally he whispered to the audience, "He took out the fiend's eye!" The gathered Pandyr listened side by side with the Bearzyrk. Ullstag was a master storyteller, and he was clearly building up to a grand finish. "It's true. He took the fiend's eye with a giant ice sickle he had taken from the heart of Icegard. It was the only thing that would not melt when it touched the skin of the fire giant king. Sumyr ran off shrieking as Ghostmane left Firehome with the giant's burning eye impaled on the ice spear, and the Bearzyrk soon forged it into a spearhead of fire. And with his weapons ready, Ghostmane—"

"He went to Icegard!" said Frostpaw.

Ullstag smiled at the boy and patted his head. "That he did . . . Frostpaw, is it? Yes, indeed, to Icegard he went. He claimed now that he had a weapon hot enough to pierce the very heart of Wintyr. He figured he would slay old Glacier Heart with his own brother's eye. Well, he eventually faced Wintyr, and the battle did rage. It was said to have lasted the entire length of Wintyr's reign, and that in Mistgard there were no snows that year. All of the energy Wintyr would normally hurl at the world was used to heal the wounds he received during the melee. No matter how hard he tried, Ghostmane could not land a killing blow. The storms of Wintyr filled in all the cracks left by the blazing spear and made his hide even thicker. All but defeated, Ghostmane fell into the snow, and Wintyr picked up his body, ready to squeeze Ghostmane to pulp. With limbs and bones cracking, Ghostmane figured out that what worked once would work again."

"No. He didn't . . ." said Frostpaw.

The Pandyr listened and waited. Frostpaw was at the point of bursting when Ullstag finally spoke. "Ghostmane took another eye!"

The crowds went wild. Mugs were downed and fists pounded tables. The Bearzyrk had heard this story too many times to count, but they seemed to be reliving it once again through Frostpaw's excitement.

"Ah, well, Wintyr howled with pain, and it was said that it stormed across the world for so long that there was snow even in Firehome. With a mighty hurl, Ghostmane was flung across the ocean to land upon the very shores of Mistgard. He was washed ashore a broken mess. He refused all aid and went immediately to his forge. There he fashioned another spear out of the eye of Wintyr, and he hung the two weapons on a set of giant white elkhorn antlers. I was told this tale by an old Bearzyrk, just like I am now telling you, Snow—Snowfoot?"

"Yes—well, what happened next?" said Frostpaw excitedly, unconcerned with correcting the Bearzyrk's mistake.

"After he hung the spears, he took nine steps backward and fell dead," said Ullstag plainly, and he took a pull from his drinking horn. The room was silent for a few moments, until Ullstag threw down his empty horn, belched, and shouted, "But what a great end for a story! Now both of these demons have but two eyes between them! And not only that, but he left the spears for future generations to use against our foes."

The old Bearzyrk stood up and gave a toast with a throaty yell. "To Ghostmane!" The other Bearzyrk raised their horns and mugs.

Byorgn snorted and folded his arms. He had taken neither food nor drink, and he had not allowed his exhausted clansmen to do so, either. "Sounds more like a child's story than fact to me."

"Sssshut your maw, you pompous, fancy-cloaked ffffool!" There was a great crashing from under the table, and Thoryn stood up and overturned it again. He raised his empty horn. "To Ghosshtmane!" he blurted out before he fell back and landed on Ullstag. Thoryn looked at the Bearzyrk with one eye closed and the other trying to focus on the old one's face. "That was a really good story . . . and good mead. Could I have—" And the chieftain of the Hammerheart fell asleep across the old Bearzyrk's lap.

"Well, old Ghostmane rests now, rests with his giants' eyes. His bones lie deep in the Den of the Slayers, in the highest seat just outside our little mountain, though only the elders, like Frostvang, are allowed to enter. Ha! They don't let us youngsters in," Ullstag said, rubbing his long white whiskers.

"So you were brought here by the Storm Speaker when you were just a boy?" said Frostpaw.

"Aye, lad, way younger than you, in fact," said the elder Jadebow. He looked around and waved his large hand toward the rest of the Bearzyrk in the hall. "We all hail from the eight clans originally. And for one reason or another, we were abandoned or cast out into the wilds. Some of us survived alone in the mountains for decades before wandering here to the Tundyr, but most of us were delivered by your Storm Speaker. The kindness of the Dark Beard saved many of us from a grim life and a lonely death." The other Bearzyrk raised their mugs and drank deeply. Ullstag drank as well. "Aye, the Dark Beard is friend to us. He has no clan himself, but it seems he is making a fine one of his own. Do you know from which clan you hail—Little Paw, is it?"

Frostpaw didn't correct the big Bearzyrk. He simply shook his head. "I do not. The Storm Speaker found me in the woods, and if he knows of my origins, he has never told me."

The old bear looked at the boy thoughtfully for a moment and spoke to him from his heart. "I want you to listen to me, Little Paw. You see, it doesn't matter where you come from. Family? Blood? Those are fine and grand, but they are not the strongest of bonds. If that were true"—he once again motioned to his Bearzyrk brethren—"then how did we all end up here? Bah, I believe the strongest of bonds come not from blood or family ties but from those forged in life. Bonds born from the battles we share, on the battlefield as well as off, bonds formed through friendship."

The gathered Bearzyrk grunted and rumbled in agreement.

"But you all come from somewhere, from some clan? Even the great Ghostmane himself must have come from one of the eight clans," said Frostpaw.

"Yes, he did, lad. Yes, he did. But just remember this: it's not where you come from or what you are born into; it's what you do with the life given to you. We are only given so many breaths in this life, you know. It is what we do in between those breaths that matters." Ullstag pointed a white-furred paw toward Ursara and Frostpaw. "The ties that are built and forged through brotherhood, through love . . . those are the strongest bonds. Blood is strong, but blood"—he held up his white arms—"blood will only go so far."

Frostpaw thought about the words the old Bearzyrk spoke, and he pulled Ursara close to his side. Both nibbled on some bread and sipped beer.

"What is the story with you both? Clearly there is no fear of our kind with you, little lady," said Ullstag.

Ursara smiled at the big Bearzyrk.

CHAPTER 15

URSARA SPEAKS

Y FATHER AND I ARE not from any clan. If our ancestors were, it has long since passed into the mists of his memory. We were all the clan we needed. So you can imagine that when Father brought Frostpaw into our family, I was beyond horrified, though not by his appearance. I was upset at how much my life had changed. No longer was I the only child in Father's world. No longer did I receive all of his affection. I remember being angry, for years, it seemed. Our little clan of two had an outsider in it. I was always looking for ways to get Frostpaw into trouble, whether it was breaking something and blaming it on him, or something else just as childish. He never told Father it was me. He always took whatever punishment there was. It made me furious, but it made me feel even more horrible for what I was doing to him. That was always his way. He bore every burden the mountain threw at him. I think for the first ten years or so, I was angry at him, but I was even angrier at myself."

She cleared her throat and blinked back the tears that welled up in her eyes. "One day, everything changed." Ursara took Frostpaw's large hand in her tiny one. "Earlier in the day, Frostpaw was out amongst the herds, as he always seemed to be when he was younger, for he knew nothing of prejudice or the other 'civilized' things we Pandyr had created. A group of our most honorable young clansmen got to teasing Frostpaw and started throwing rocks and sticks at him, calling him names. You know how we can be. Well, they did their worst to him, and as always, he accepted it." Ursara's eyes misted up at the thought, but soon they were dried by anger. "These cowards surrounded Frostpaw and doused him with pitch! They wanted to make his color more to their liking. I believe they would have gotten away with all their fun had they left it at that. But one of them, as he was laughing at Frostpaw, took up a rock, and instead of hitting Frostpaw, he hit one of the elkhorn he ran with. The herd scattered, with the exception of the one that was hit. That one lay bleeding and still. What happened next was Frostpa—"

"Ursara, please, don't," said Frostpaw. He looked at her with pleading eyes.

"No, you can't stop there!" said Ullstag. "It sounds like there's going to be a right thrashing served out! Come on, lad, let her finish the story."

Ursara gently nodded at Frostpaw. "No, I won't tell the details. I will say that Father had plenty to deal with when he returned to Thunder's Home that evening. There must have been twenty angry mothers and fathers, all foaming at the maw, trying to find out why the Storm Speaker's boy attacked their little darlings. Ha! Poor Father just sat there and tried to calm them all down. Nothing worked until Frostpaw came from the forest, carrying the wounded elk in his arms. He was still covered in tar, and he had found a wrap for the elk so she wouldn't be fouled by the stinking pitch they had doused him with.

"You could have heard a feather drop when he walked by the families of our noble clansmen. They all looked to their youngsters, some with shame and some with indifference. When Father saw what they had done to Frostpaw, he glared at the gathered clansmen, and lightning flashed above, followed so quickly by thunder that everyone jumped out of their skins. His ire was about to boil over when Frostpaw spoke. All he said was, 'She needs help,' motioning to the elk. Well, that seemed to end the day's events. Frostpaw and Father helped out the elk, and none of the clan boys ever bothered Frostpaw again."

"Well done, lad," said Ullstag, and a few other Bearzyrk raised their mugs. "I'll bet a few of them are here tonight as well, eh?" he said softly as he eyed Byorgn and his Sunspear. Ullstag had seen the disdain in the chieftain's eyes upon first meeting him on the Tundyr.

Frostpaw saw the looks that passed between the two, and he desperately tried to change the subject. "You, uh, earlier you mentioned that all the Bearzyrk came from one of the original eight clans, even this Ghostmane. Do all the Bearzyrk here know of their origins?" Frostpaw looked around the room at the Bearzyrk, who shook their shaggy manes.

Ullstag stood and stretched his old bones. "Like I said, boy, this is our clan now. It doesn't matter where we were from, only that we are here now," he said jovially, and he raised a horn to the room. He motioned for Frostpaw to grab a tankard. "Raise one with us, lad. You are one of us and can stay here if you wish."

Ursara grabbed a mug and handed it to Frostpaw, who hesitantly held it up. The Bearzyrk and Frostpaw drank while the Pandyr clansmen watched in silence. Wiping a paw across his maw, Frostpaw gently set down the mug and lowered his head. "Thank you, Ullstag, for the friendship and the offer. But I will be staying with my clan, the Storm Speaker and Ursara. Like you said, the strongest bonds are not from blood or clan but from the ties built up out of friendship and love."

"Well said, boy," said the Bearzyrk as he picked up his bow and patted it fondly.

"So what clan did thish great Ghoshtmane hail from? It sounds like he would clearly be from the Hammerheart, if the stories of his battle prowess be true," said Thoryn groggily as he sat up. He crawled across the floor, looking for a tankard amongst the broken mugs and cups. Frostpaw extended a hand to the bearded chieftain. Thoryn slapped his red paw into the center of Frostpaw's big white one, and he was hoisted up to standing.

Ullstag scratched his great head and thought for a moment. "My memory isn't all that it used to be. He was not of the Hammerheart, though. I believe the great one was originally of the Sunspe—"

"Shut your maw, you frost-bitten dog!"

CHAPTER 16
TAKING SIDES

THE ROOM TURNED TO see Byorgn, chieftain of the Sunspear, overturn a table. "You'll not dishonor the Sunspear name while Byorgn draws air! You wag your tongue about how blood and family do not matter! What do you know of family and blood? You were not wanted. Your births were a shame on your clans! Now you try to scar the great family of the Sunspear by saying your pale dog of a champion was of the same blood as I?"

The Sunspear chieftain charged and hit Ullstag with a mighty swing that started from the floor and ended against the old Bearzyrk's jaw, snapping back his great maw. The Bearzyrk shook off the blow and retaliated with a brutal backhanded swipe that sent the chieftain sailing into his fellow clansmen. The other Bearzyrk, seeing one of their own attacked, roared. The Sunspear clansmen drew weapons and charged with their chieftain, whose golden spear was hungry for blood. They were stopped by a small figure.

"Enough!" said the daughter of the Storm Speaker. Her normally quiet voice echoed in the hall like a soft thunder shock. Ullstag and Byorgn were both brought to a halt mere feet from each other. Only the tiny Ursara stood between the two massive beings. "Chieftain, please. We are not at war here.

Do not dishonor us by raising arms against our hosts. Surely there is—"

Ursara was abruptly silenced by the thick, hairy paw of Byorgn cuffing her across the cheek. "You dare speak to me of honor? The way you consort with that white-furred mongrel? You disgrace the entirety of the eight clans by—"

There was a guttural roar, and Byorgn's words were not merely cut off; they were strangled shut. He was lifted off of his feet by burly white arms. The arms were not those of the old Ullstag but of the young Frostpaw. A murderous blue mist swirled in Frostpaw's inner vision. In the back of his mind, he could hear dark words being whispered to him.

Kill . . . slay . . . MURDER.

But the sinister voice was replaced with another. It was soft and gentle, in direct contrast to the voice of icy-blue madness. "Frostpaw, do not do this. I beg you," pleaded Ursara.

The boy shook his head, trying to rid it of the rage that burned in his mind. He let go of the Sunspear chieftain, who crashed to the cavern floor in a heap. Byorgn lay still but soon coughed and sputtered, rubbing his bruised throat. He rose unsteadily with the help of his clansmen. When he gained his footing, he stalked forward, bloodlust in his eyes.

"How dare you, you fatherless dog! You take sides with them instead of your own ki—" The Sunspear stopped midstride and midsentence, laughing cruelly. "Of course you side with these cursed wretches; these are your kind. You were never one of us. No matter how hard you try or how close you are to the Storm Speaker, you will never be one of us!"

"That much we can agree on. I will never be one of your kind," said Frostpaw.

After the Sunspear clansmen removed themselves to a corner to tend to their battered leader, Frostpaw remembered Ursara. "Are you hurt?" he said.

"I am not, but you are bleeding from the mouth. Were you hit?" The youth put his paw to his face and felt blood trickling from his mouth. He arched his lips and bared his fangs for Ursara, who was looking for a wound or cut. "Your fangs, Frostpaw. It cannot be." Ursara's voice had a quiver of worry to it.

"Yes, it can be, lass," said Ullstag as he came over to the two. "We Bearzyrk have a tendency to change a bit in times of anger or in times of need. It is a curse and a gift we embrace. We all change eventually. Change to something

84

more primal, more basic. There are tales of our kind falling so far to the ice lord's taunting that they turn into pure beasts, no longer walking on two legs but running on all four. Did you hear the voice, Frostpaw?"

Frostpaw looked around the room and shook his head.

"It's all right, lad. You are not alone. We all hear the voice; we all hear it." The old bear fell silent and withdrew.

The Sunspear chieftain gathered up his clan and hollered orders at the top of his lungs. To the rest, he said, "The Sunspear are leaving this den of cursed beasts! Better to die amongst the giants than to risk our lives with this lot. The Storm Speaker has failed us all, thinking that these dogs would be able to aid us in our darkest days."

ULLSTAG

CHAPTER 17
INTO THE STORM

THE SUNSPEAR CLAN MADE ready to leave the cavernous hall of the Bearzyrk while the Storm Speaker and Frostvang stood to the side. They, too, had seen the exchange, and they were tired and filled with sadness. Close behind them mocked the grizzled Grymir.

"You see, Storm Speaker? Our kinds can never be together for long. You cast us out, and when we welcome you into our halls, your people seek bloodshed. I think it is time for all the Pandyr clans to follow the Sunspear."

"Elder Grymir," pleaded Frostvang, "I promised the clans food and shelter for at least the night."

"You do not have the authority to offer such things, Frostvang. If you wish to provide food and lodging, I guess you should go help them find some," he snarled. He turned to the Storm Speaker with a grimace. "Goodbye, Storm Speaker. This will be our last meeting in this life." Then old Grymir turned to join his fellow Bearzyrk in the hall, and he spoke no more to Frostvang or the Storm Speaker.

The two stood outside the cavern with the Pandyr clans as they gathered their herds. The Bearzyrk seemed to have mixed emotions about the situation, but they did as the council told them. Swiftly and without a word, they helped the Pandyr and their mounts move out.

The winds were roaring and blowing like mad, and snow fell in sheets. But none of that mattered to Byorgn. "The Sunspear are leaving, Storm Speaker. You and your pale-skinned devils can go on your own. We will not linger in the presence of the cursed any longer. We'd rather die in Wintyr's breath than amidst treacherous—"

"Please, Chieftain," said Frostvang, "I know a place where all can stay. It is near an area sacred to the Bearzyrk. None go there; none will bother you. I will send a guide to take you there."

The Sunspear chieftain eyed Frostvang warily.

"A guide?" the Storm Speaker said. "So you are to stay here, then, Frostvang?"

"I am, Dark Beard. I will attempt to reason with the council. I believe there will be little I can do, but I must try." He looked over at Frostpaw and Ursara. "You are welcome to join me, Frostpaw. I would like a moment to talk to you about some things."

Frostpaw stood in the ripping wind, unaffected by the storm. "I do not wish to talk now, Frostvang. I am sorry, but I need . . ." He trailed off and was silent. Ursara came up and put her arms around him, and he held her close.

The old bear nodded and patted the youngster on his white-maned head. "Very well, Frostpaw. Perhaps we can speak tomorrow when I bring news about the council's decision. Either way, tomorrow we will know how to proceed."

The Sunspear chieftain snorted, spat, and returned to his clansmen. He spoke with them briefly and looked back at the Storm Speaker with a curt nod. It seemed as if, for the moment, the Sunspear would stay.

The Storm Speaker and Frostvang stood in silence, looking at the sky. "It seems both sides share something in common, Frostvang . . . We are too set in our ways to change. Something needs to happen soon, for Wintyr is here," said the Storm Speaker.

"He is, Dark Beard," said Frostvang grimly. "His whispers grow stronger with every storm cloud . . . I hear them. So does Frostpaw. I will talk to him tomorrow about everything. Tomorrow he will know all."

Ullstag rode up on a spearhorn, bow in hand.

"Ullstag knows the way to the shelter. He will lead you there. Till tomorrow, Dark Beard." Frostvang turned and departed into the cave.

Ullstag's enormous frame filled the cavern's opening as he spoke loudly over the wind. "Follow me! I know of a place where we will find shelter from this miserable night." He shifted his considerable bulk and adjusted a large keg he had tethered to the poor beast laboring under his gigantic girth. "I brought some of my mead as well, to help against the cold." And with a smile, he reined his spearhorn and plunged into the storm.

***

Ullstag led the eight clans a few miles away from the great hall where the Bearzyrk made their home. Ice and fire fell like dying stars across the Tundyr as they rode farther and farther into the storm. Soon the clans noticed strange obelisks and monoliths similar in form to the ones they had seen in the Circle in the Sky, though these were not made of stone and wood. These monoliths looked to be made of solid crystalline ice, and at the center of the formation was a giant cairn. The Pandyr rode by it in silence, looking with suspicion at the strange blue twin of their own circle back home.

Frostpaw.

The youth looked up to see who was talking to him. It was not the sinister voice he would hear distantly in his mind, the one that raged and urged him to kill. No, this voice he did not recognize, though something was familiar about it. As the boy lowered his head again, the voice returned.

Frostpaw.

The voice was not filled with anger or violent aggression; the voice he heard was strong and deep, and it resonated in his mind. He shook his head and looked at the Storm Speaker and Ullstag. "Did you say something to me just then?" said Frostpaw.

The Storm Speaker and Ullstag eyed each other strangely. "No, lad, but the old circle we just passed may have something to do with it," said the Bearzyrk.

Frostpaw looked over and saw the columns of ice and the tomb that stood in the center. "What is it? Is it similar to our Circle in the Sky?"

Ullstag answered the boy in a reverent tone. "We Bearzyrk have many traditions that we carried with us from our clans long ago. This area is known as the Circle of the Fallen. It is our burial site for our long-lost brothers. See the mound in the center? That is what we call the Den of the Slayers."

"The Den of the Slayers," said Frostpaw dreamily.

89

"It is a place of rest. Inside the icy walls lie the bones of our greatest warriors. It is said that, to some, they speak. I've never heard anything in all my years, though. The council has forbidden us to enter. Ah, look here; we are close." The old bear rode on silently and soon called for everyone to listen. "There, just ahead in the mountainside, is a series of caves large enough to hold your clans for the night, though the animals will need to stay outside if you all are to fit," said Ullstag.

Frostpaw walked as if in a trance, and the Storm Speaker saw the worry in Ursara's eyes. He put his hand on hers and gave it a squeeze. "He will be all right, Ursara. He has been through an awful lot today. Give him time to think," the Storm Speaker said softly.

She followed Frostpaw, and they went off together. The Storm Speaker watched them with fondness.

"Storm Speaker!" shouted the Hammerheart chieftain.

Jolted from his thoughts, the Storm Speaker rode swiftly to Thoryn. "What is it? Are the giants upon us?"

The chieftain shook his head. "Not giants, though I think this is almost as bad," he said grimly.

"Well . . . what is it, then?"

Thoryn whispered to the Storm Speaker. "It is the Sunspear clan. They are gone."

CHAPTER 18

IN SEARCH OF
THE SUNSPEAR

HE REMAINING SEVEN CLANS were silent. The Storm Speaker sat stiffly on Traveler, contemplating the situation. The Hammerheart chieftain was astounded. "How did an entire clan leave our group without our knowing? What's worse is that in this blizzard, an army of giants could have walked up on us and taken them, and we still wouldn't have known!"

Ullyr rode up on Dawnstrider and reined her in. "With this wind and sleet, it is no wonder we didn't see anything. Even the Jadebow missed this. I fear had we not stopped for shelter, we could have gone the whole night without noticing."

The Storm Speaker turned and faced the group. "The circle is breaking . . . . We have no way of surviving without the Sunspear's and the Bearzyrk's might. We must get every Pandyr and Bearzyrk to unite if our people are to survive. Alone, on our own . . ." The Storm Speaker trailed off.

Ullstag spoke. "I know these flatlands well; I know the places to seek shelter. I will go find them. It can't be too hard. A whole clan cannot just disappear! At least, not from this old sniffer," he said, placing a long, clawed finger next to his weather-worn nose.

"You'd better not go, old one," said Ullyr. "Byorgn is barely peaceable to his own kind. I wouldn't put it past him and his clan to attack you in vengeance for the night's earlier events. It is better that my fleetest riders and I go. As you say, it is a whole clan. Even in this weather, it shouldn't be too hard for a Jadebow to track them."

Thoryn rode up awkwardly on his elkhorn. "And the Hammerheart will send its finest hammerers to aid you. There are giants about, you know."

The Jadebow chose his words carefully. "Nay, Chieftain, I must decline your offer. On this night we must ride swiftly, and we must ride silently. You and your Hammerheart are not the riders that the Jadebow are." Thoryn started to protest, but Ullyr put his hand up to quell the red one's ire. "Just as the Jadebow are not the warriors that the Hammerheart are. Were this a stand-up fight, there is no other clan I would want by my side."

The Hammerheart nodded his head and chuckled. "You are right. The Hammerheart will wait here and let the Jadebow do what they do best." Thoryn thrust out his reddish paw, and Ullyr's tawny paw joined it in a shake.

"Watch my clan for me till I get back, will you?" the Jadebow said with a grin.

"Aye, I will," said Thoryn. "Just so long as you watch your back. We need your arrows, you old jaegyr hound! Go! Ride swiftly, my friend." Thoryn swatted Dawnstrider hard on her rump, and the golden elkhorn snorted and jostled her reins. Then the Jadebow chief and eight of his riders were off.

After a few moments, the Pandyr were in the caves, preparing for the night. Watches were set, and what little rations remained were halved again and devoured. Ullstag rode up to the Storm Speaker. He was about to speak when he was abruptly hushed by the Dark Beard.

"Please make sure Ullyr and his riders return. We don't dare lose Ullyr as well."

The old Bearzyrk laughed. "I'll bring him back, Dark Beard. Don't you worry. I won't lose them on the same day I found them." And with that, Ullstag turned and went into the storm.

92

CHAPTER 19

THE NINE DAUGHTERS
OF THE STORM SPEAKER

HE NIGHT GREW. THE STORM outside was unrelenting, and the bitter cold was grueling to those trying to find sleep in the caves. The only comfort they could muster was that it must be warmer here than where Ullyr and his brave riders were.

The Storm Speaker sat at the front of the cave, oblivious to the weather. Frostpaw sat sullenly across the chamber. "Why did you not tell me there were more like me, Father? My whole life, I was alone, an outcast to everyone save you and Ursara. Had I known there were more like me, I . . ." He trailed off.

The boy was almost in tears, and this tore deeply into the Storm Speaker's heart. He walked over to Frostpaw and sat next to him. "Did you know that I had a daughter before Ursara, Frostpaw?" Frostpaw wiped his face and shook his head. "I actually had many daughters over many years. And all of them were beautiful; all were perfect. They grew into fine Pandyr."

Frostpaw sat up straight and looked at the old one. "Where are they now?" he said. "How come I have never met them before?"

The old one looked at Frostpaw with such sorrow that the boy started to cry. "Frostpaw, the reason that you have never met them is . . ." The Storm

93

Speaker shook his head and wiped the tears forming at the corners of his eyes. "The reason is that they all are gone."

"Gone? Gone where?" The boy felt stupid as soon as he said it.

"They have long passed from this realm and now travel the realms of another world, if there is one," the Storm Speaker said grimly.

"Oh," was all Frostpaw could think to say. "I'm sorry, Storm Speaker."

"To one such as me, the happiness that love brings is merely a counterpart to the sorrow it leaves. It is something that I have long learned to live with. I would meet a fine woman. Eventually we would fall in love, and then, as it happens, we would have a cub. Eventually the wives would tire of my ways and leave me for some far more stable Pandyr. I never blamed them. But the cubs, the cubs always wanted to stay with me."

He smiled at the memory, and Frostpaw wished that he, too, could see these children of the Storm Speaker.

"Ah, my little girls. I always had girls. I would watch them grow, and eventually I would watch them marry." He looked outside at the roaring storm, lost in thought. "For some reason, they could never have little ones of their own. They would grow old, and eventually they would die. I have buried eight of my cubs, Frostpaw." The old man started to choke up. "I have buried my eight little girls whom I brought into this world. I've had to watch them all die." He looked back to where Ursara was leading their mounts down a side cavern, and he spoke softly. "Just as I will watch Ursara die one day. I will bury her, too, next to her sisters. My daughters were eight before Ursara; she is my ninth, my last one."

The old Pandyr took a deep breath and smiled a bit. "When I found you, I was immediately impressed with your heart. You were such a sweet child for one supposedly born under a bad omen." The Storm Speaker waved his hand as if dismissing the notion. "Bah! You have been a wonderful son to me. I've had many nights when I tore myself apart for not telling you of the Bearzyrk. You see, I grew to love you very much, as much as any of my own blood. I'd never had a son, Frostpaw, and for some reason, this island gave me the opportunity. There was always the thought that one day I would take you to them, but the longer we were together, the more I could not bear delivering you to the Bearzyrk as I had done with so many others. I thought that, of all my children, you would be the one who would grow old with me. With the long lives of the Bearzyrk, I figured that I would not have to bury another of my children. And I am growing old as well. It was some comfort to know that when I passed from this realm, someone would be there to see me off. Someone whom time would not take from me so easily. I was being selfish, and I am sorry, my dear, dear Frostpaw."

The boy felt grief well up in the Storm Speaker, and he moved to his side. "I will always be with you, Storm Speaker, and with Ursara. You are my family, and should the time come for you to bury—to do that again, I will be there to grieve with you." Frostpaw hugged the Storm Speaker with his powerful arms. "Good night, Storm Speaker."

The Storm Speaker hugged the lad back. "Good night, my boy."

Frostpaw smiled and left to find Ursara.

Had father or son known that this would be the last exchange between them, neither would have changed a single word.

CHAPTER 20

LAKE OF FIRE

LLYR AND HIS RIDERS rode steadily across the Tundyr. The storms of ice and ember made seeing difficult, but Ullyr's keen senses managed to pick up the Sunspear's trail. Even the tracks of an entire clan were nearly obliterated by the roaring winds. Suddenly, Ullyr breathed deeply and chuckled. He held his arm high, hand clenched in a fist, and his riders stopped. The breaths of both mounts and riders froze in the air.

"We have company," said the Jadebow chieftain.

Some distance behind them, a figure emerged from the driving storm. Ullyr laughed, and the Jadebow waited for their visitor. From the swirling darkness, Ullstag, all eight hundred pounds of him, appeared through the snow, riding a laboring spearhorn. "The storm is strong. See how my noble steed wearies under its force?" The old bear heaved up his keg and took a tremendous pull from the barrel, wiping away the froth from his beard. "Care for a nip? I threw in a few bits of the Dark Beard's honeycomb for added punch."

"No mead for us, Ullstag. We must find the Sunspear, though I grow worried at the chances of finding them in this storm. It appears that the tracks stop here, at this frozen lake."

97

Ullstag tapped the lake's icy crust with his bow and urged his spearhorn across the surface, not allowing the big beast much room for protest. "Don't worry. This old ice is a foot thick at the thinnest points; it'll hold. Mind your goats, though. Their hooves were not made to traverse this terrain as easily as a spearhorn's."

The Jadebow exchanged leery looks with one another. "Do you have any idea where you're going? Where do you think they are, Ullstag?" asked Ullyr.

"I know of some old fishing lodges that we use when land food isn't available. Another mile or so, we will be upon them. If I were a wandering clan caught in a whirlwind of ice and fire, those little huts would seem like a mother's arms. Come, follow Ullstag."

The Pandyr watched for a moment, unsure what to do. Ullyr patted Dawnstrider and coaxed her forward onto the ice. The others looked skeptical but followed suit. Though at first their hooves skated and slid, the fleet-footed elkhorn soon traversed the frosty ice as though it were their own rocky hills. They continued on into the blackening night until suddenly Ullstag motioned for the riders to halt. He sniffed the air and grunted in disgust. He looked at his fellow Jadebow and grimaced.

"Giants," he said reproachfully. The old bear drew one of his sapling-sized arrows out of his quiver. It was then that howls could be heard through the ripping wind. Howls that were born not from storm, ice, or fire, but from living throats. Though the words were lost to the winds, their tone was clear: They were the wails of the dying mixed with the sound of battle.

"The Sunspear!" said Ullyr. He nocked his arrow and charged forward.

***

The caves were silent except for a few embers that popped from dying fires and the occasional snore of the weary. The only other sound was that of the wind as it moaned through the cavern like a spirit of frost. Frostpaw wandered his way through the caves until he found where Ursara was. Having no large clan to worry about, Ursara had found a spot large enough to house both Traveler and Cinder, as well as a small alcove for herself and Frostpaw. Knowing the ways of her father, Ursara doubted the Storm Speaker would move from his watch at the cave's mouth. The cold was somewhat abated in the hollow she had chosen, thanks to the pools of warm mineral water that dotted the cavern floor. Ursara tended a small fire and had it glowing brightly in the corner when Frostpaw entered and sat down, his large body taking up as much room as the elk, it seemed.

"How are you, Frostpaw? Much has happened today. It must weigh heavily on your mind. All this time Father knew about the Bearzyrk, and he never told you," she said quietly.

Frostpaw knew the reason for his father's actions. He would tell her eventually, but for now he sat in silence.

"I can't imagine what you must be going through. Everything we have known is gone." Anger started to fill her eyes. "We war with each other?" Ursara wiped tears that were swiftly falling down her cheeks. "And what happened to you, Frostpaw, in the cave with Byorgn? Your fangs, the blood? What happened to you tonight?" She walked a few steps away, trying in vain to hide her tears.

Frostpaw rose and put his arms around Ursara's small shoulders. "Even after all that has happened, nothing has really changed." His voice was steady and calm. "I am still looked upon as an outcast, an ill omen, by the clans." He laughed softly. "Even more so now by the Sunspear. But that doesn't matter." He turned Ursara around to face him, her eyes still wet. He touched his maw, gently probing the incisors that protruded farther than they had in the early morning. "This change has happened to me before, Ursara, and it appears that it is likely to happen again."

Ursara looked confused, but before she could speak, she was quieted by a gesture from Frostpaw.

"When you were telling the story tonight about the kids and—and what happened when they, you know, pushed me . . . you didn't tell them what happened afterward. You don't even know. Something happened to me that day that only the Storm Speaker and I know about. If you remember, I was gone for a few days." It was Frostpaw's turn to look away. "You probably thought I was off running like a fool again in the woods, but I wasn't."

Ursara listened to Frostpaw, who was now speaking more to himself than to her.

"I wasn't running; I couldn't have if I had wanted to. After carrying the elkhorn to the Storm Speaker for help, I—I collapsed. I could barely move. I lay in bed for days, drifting in and out of reality. All the while, I heard that voice whispering to me things of violence and slaughter. I don't recall much of it. But when I could walk again, the Storm Speaker and I both noticed immediately."

Ursara stood quietly. The small fire made Frostpaw's shadow look like a gigantic ghost on the cavern wall. With a gasp, she spoke. "You changed— I remember now! You looked not just taller but larger all around."

Frostpaw turned and held Ursara gently. "When their words and stones were hitting me, I could deal with that. I have grown up dealing with pain and hurt." He placed his hand on the side of Ursara's face, cradling it. "But when the stones were cast at something . . . someone I cared for, I forgot everything other than to stop whatever was hurting her." Frostpaw took Ursara's hand in his own. They looked at each other for long moments, and the uncomfortable youth who was normally Frostpaw seemed not to be in the cave that night. "The world is in chaos and on the edge of destruction, and I am still hated by the clans. Nothing has changed for me because the most important things in my life are still with me."

He slowly released Ursara and walked over to where the elkhorn dozed. "My oldest companion, Traveler, is still with me." The gray elkhorn snorted as Frostpaw petted her affectionately. He pointed toward the entrance of their small alcove. "The only father I have ever known is still here with me, watching over the clans." Frostpaw walked back to Ursara and stopped just short of her small frame. "And the most important person in my little clan of four is still with me. You, you are still with me. Knowing that, I can bear any burden I am given."

Ursara closed the span between them, and her arms wrapped around him. He held her with a grip that is given only to the first love of one's life. The act of concealing their feelings—from each other, from the Storm Speaker, from the clans, and even from themselves—was abandoned with their first kiss.

***

Ullyr and his men charged across the frozen lake's surface, sending up flutters of ice and snow. The elkhorn frothed at the mouth, frost coating their muzzles as they labored through the storm. The din of battle roared on, and the riders surveyed the scene that appeared before them.

The Sunspear clan was embattled by frost and firekin. The Pandyr parried axes of ice and swords of glowing iron, and many bodies from both sides littered the surface of the frozen lake. The storm was making the fight all the more difficult, but the size of the giantkin made them easy targets for the Jadebow clansmen. The riders, on Ullyr's command, nocked green wooden arrows into bows of hardened yew and let loose a hurricane of

razor-barbed death upon the giantkin. Bodies dropped like dead trees upon the crimson-slick ice, and cheers rang up from the Sunspear.

Emboldened by the arrival of their allies, the Sunspear tightened their ranks and formed a wall of death, bristling with spears, pikes, and javelins with which they impaled the charging giantkin. The Jadebow released another wave of devastation upon their foes, peppering red and blue hides with deadly feathers of green.

"Hail Sunspear!" yelled Ullyr and his riders.

"Welcome to the battle, Jadebow!" Byorgn yelled back with a throat hoarse from screaming. The Sunspear chieftain looked battered and beaten, but he still stood his ground.

"I think they are pulling back. Look, they run to the forests. Loose another volley, my archers!" shouted Ullyr.

Ullstag launched another spear-sized arrow that impaled two giantkin together. Suddenly he noticed something peculiar. "Is it dawn already?" muttered the Bearzyrk.

Ullyr looked at the dim light glowing eerily over the tree line. "Only if the golden skull rises from the south. What treachery is at hand?" His answer came a moment later.

From out of the frozen forest came the living Son of Fire himself. Oak and pine trees burned as he walked through them as though they were mere blades of grass. The giantkin slowly moved back into the forest as their lord and master, King Sumyr, broke the tree line and stood facing the Sunspear and Jadebow clans. He was easily thirty feet tall, dwarfing all but the tallest of trees, and his skin was a bloody copper hue, pocked with basalt and obsidian shards. He wore blackened iron plate and ring mail that glowed from the heat, and his beard was an inferno of flame. Atop his head floated a massive crown of iron and fire. He towered above the Sunspear chieftain as a mountain does a stone.

The king of Firehome laughed wickedly and produced a large sword that he carried across his back. The sound of it being unsheathed was that of a thousand forges igniting at once. The iron sword blazed a crimson red and burst into flame as he raised it above his head. Magma dripped from the twenty-foot blade like poison from a serpent's fang. The icy lake's surface began to melt and crack, and Ullyr and his riders backed away, sensing the imminent conclusion to this encounter.

"Get off the ice! Retreat, retreat!" Ullyr yelled frantically.

Those close to fallen Sunspear helped the wounded onto their elkhorn. Ullstag rode up to the Sunspear leader, arm extended. "Come, Chieftain. The battle is lost. We must run."

Byorgn glared at the Bearzyrk and shouted back in rage, "Get away from me, you white demon!" He raised his broken spear with murderous intent when the sword of Sumyr smashed down upon the frozen lake.

There was a hissing mist of white-hot steam followed by a blast of boiling water. The surface cracked, and the lake became a spider web of jagged shards of ice. Ullyr and his men had scarcely been able to turn and run when they felt the ground giving way beneath them.

"Run like never before, Dawnstrider! Run for our lives!" shouted Ullyr. Dawnstrider and the rest of the elkhorn barreled across the cracking surface. Ullyr looked back at Ullstag, whose spearhorn was no match for the swiftness of the elkhorn.

"Run, little chieftain. I'll meet you—"

Ullyr saw the giant Bearzyrk and his mount fall through the broken lake, the hole quickly covered up by melting chunks of ice. There was a ripping sound, almost like that of stone being torn apart. Beneath the hooves of Dawnstrider, Ullyr saw a white crack dance below the surface of the ice like a bolt of lightning. He looked to his men and to Dawnstrider as the ice splintered, fractured, and gave way to the boiling water underneath.

Ullyr and his riders fell into the roiling blackness of the burning lake.

CHAPTER 21

HEARTS AND ORIGINS

FROSTPAW.

The youth awoke from a sound sleep. Ursara lay curled in his arms, and the fire was nothing but embers. Frostpaw closed his eyes and listened to the wind whisper.

Frostpaw.

This time he stood up. Ursara woke as well and looked around the cave. "What is it, Frostpaw?" she said.

"Did you hear that? I heard my name."

Ursara blinked sleepily and lay back amongst the quilted blankets, wrapping herself up against the chill. "Maybe it was Father calling for you," she said as she started to drift back to sleep.

Nodding to himself, Frostpaw knelt down and went under the blankets again, thinking of the Storm Speaker. *I should go check on him. It is cold and late, and this journey has taken its toll.*

He was just asleep when he heard the voice again.

Frostpaw.

This time, the voice did not startle him. Instead, he sat there silently and listened.

Where the warriors sleep and dream, I would speak.

That was neither the Storm Speaker nor the wind, thought Frostpaw. He kissed Ursara lightly on the head. "I'll be back. I'm going to check on the Storm Speaker."

Ursara rolled over, put her hand on his face, and looked gently upon him. "You are sweet to care for him so." She sat up and removed a thin braided cord from around her neck. Dangling from the necklace was a small reddish gem that glowed from deep within. "I wish for you to have this, Frostpaw."

Frostpaw shook his head slowly. "Ursara, no, I cannot. That was your mother's. She meant for you to have it."

"Indeed, it was my mother's. Before that, it was Father's. He gave it to her, and when my mother died, she left this to me. And now, I give it to you." Ursara deftly untied the fastener and tried to put the necklace around Frostpaw's neck, but the cord was too small. She tied it around his wrist.

Frostpaw held up his arm and looked at the gem, frowning. The gemstone, normally a vibrant red, seemed dull and empty of light. "What happened to the light within? It seems to—"

"Watch, Frostpaw." Ursara and Frostpaw stood close together, and she pressed the stone to his wrist. They watched the tiny gem go from dormant darkness to a ruddy red, and he felt a gentle warmth slowly spread up from his wrist. "This is called a heart stone. It is just a simple stone, but when it's held over a warm hearth or body, the stone absorbs the heat, and the elements within the gem glow. Father said that the Under-King's realm is full of them, every size and color imaginable."

"It's beautiful, Ursara," said Frostpaw as he pulled her close. He placed his hand upon hers and thought for a moment. He took up a length of his white hair, braided it quickly, and with a flick of his claw, cut it loose. He looked around and found a suitable bit of wood from the fire and set to work, carving away at it till the wood resembled a crude heart. He bound the braid and wooden heart together, making a simple necklace and charm. With a few more scrapes, Frostpaw engraved the wood with his rune symbol. It was not the work of a master jeweler by any means, but it was a heart forged from the heart. He placed the braid around Ursara's neck, and the charm hung just above her chest.

She looked at him and smiled, speaking softly in the quiet cave. "Wherever you go, Frostpaw, my heart goes with you."

"And wherever I go, my heart stays with you," Frostpaw said.

He silently walked out of their small cave. Traveler stood quietly as he went past. "We're not leaving now, old friend. Rest awhile longer. I'll be back soon," he said as he stroked the dappled gray's mane.

Frostpaw wound his way through the twisting caves. Bodies were strewn wherever the ground provided space. He vaguely noted that there were still no Sunspear among the sleeping Pandyr, and he felt a pang of guilt. He saw the mouth of the cave yawn before him, where his father still sat at his vigil. Frostpaw crept over to the Storm Speaker and smiled. The old Pandyr slept silently and deeply. His cloak had fallen around his feet, and Frostpaw took it up and laid it over him once more.

Frostpaw began to head back toward where Ursara lay, but he stopped and slowly turned to the cave entrance. Snow and ash blew in and covered the floor in icy grime. He stood for a moment, gazing at the snowfall, and suddenly walked out into the storm. Ice and snow fell all around him, coating him in a layer of frost. He looked into the storm and then at the cave that led back to Ursara.

"Frostpaw?"

The youth started and whirled around. From out of the storm, a giant silhouette emerged, and through the wind and sleet, Frostpaw was able to identify the burly figure. "Frostvang, over here."

The Bearzyrk rode up and dismounted. He shook a blanket of snow off his hide, and it fell in heavy clumps to the ground. "So what brings you out into the storm when the warmth of the cave looks so inviting?" Frostvang said.

Frostpaw tried to provide an answer that would not make him sound completely crazy, but he kept stumbling over his words. "I woke up and heard something, so I figured it was . . . But he was asleep and—"

Frostvang nodded and held up his hand. "I understand."

Frostpaw was confused. "You understand?"

Frostvang put his hands on the boy's shoulders and looked at him intently. "He spoke to you, didn't he, lad? He spoke your name."

Frostpaw shook his head. "Who speaks to me? I have heard my name whispered on the winds since we got to these caves, even before, when we passed the . . ." Frostpaw's words trailed off, and he looked back at the storm.

"Come, lad, we will ride. The news I bring is nothing different than we expected. The council refuses to join with the eight clans. That news can wait till dawn. Let us give your father rest for a few more hours. We must ride and talk."

The old bear mounted his spearhorn and put his arm out. He pulled the boy up with him, and they went off into the storm. After a short distance, Frostvang spoke. "The Bearzyrk were all born from one of the eight clans, Frostpaw, though many of our kind forget or choose not to remember. As you saw today with old Ullstag, there are still those who remember their past. Most don't, but I remember. I remember well." Frostvang pulled off his cloak pin and handed it to Frostpaw. The boy turned it over and inspected the beaten brass brooch. It was a crudely carved disk that looked like a sun. The brass fastening pin was the shape of a war spear.

Frostpaw looked at the Bearzyrk in shock. "You are from the Sunspear clan?"

"Aye, lad," said Frostvang, turning slowly to the boy. "As are you."

Frostpaw felt as if he had been hit with a warhammer. He sat dazed for a moment, and the brooch he was holding fell into the snow. He leapt off of the spearhorn and dug through the snow till he found it. He brushed off the brooch as tears fell and froze on his face. Frostvang dismounted and stood beside the boy, who handed the pin back to him. "I am no Sunspear. The Sunspear have never been family to me. They have cursed me and beaten me since I was a cub. I would sooner be dead than be part of them!" Frostpaw's face bore both rage and grief.

Frostvang donned his cloak pin and adjusted it proudly. "Do not think of the Sunspear as what they have become, but what they once represented, what the Sunspear were before they became the weak-minded fools they are today. Nowadays they are led by that pompous, hate-cloaked half-chieftain. But back in the days of old, we were led by the greatest chieftain there ever was, the greatest of the Pandyr as well as the greatest of our kind. It is from his blood we truly are born."

"Who is this you speak of, Frostvang?" said Frostpaw.

Frostvang leapt upon the spearhorn and held out his hand to Frostpaw. "The one who calls you this night. Come. We will go see him."

Frostpaw took the Bearzyrk's hand and mounted behind him on the massive beast. The spearhorn lumbered forward, undaunted by the storm, carrying both elder and youth many miles to their final destination. The Circle of the Fallen stood stoically against the predawn sky, and in the center of it was the ice-bound Den of the Slayers. Frostpaw and Frostvang dismounted, walked to the den, and stood in front of a large slab of rock. Frostvang stepped to the door and gave it an immense push, but he could not budge it.

"Come here, lad, and put your shoulder to this thing," he said to Frostpaw, beckoning to him.

Frostpaw came up, shaking his head. "Ullstag says only the elders are allowed into the den," he said worriedly.

The old bear nodded his head. "They are, lad . . . and so are those who are invited."

Frostpaw bent his shoulder and put his weight into the effort. Between the two pale giants, frost cracked and shattered as the stone door moved to one side. A gust of air that smelled ancient yet somehow familiar escaped the old den and washed over the young Bearzyrk.

Frostpaw, the spectral voice said.

"I heard the voice again! Frostvang, did you hear it?"

Frostvang smiled and shook his head.

"Who speaks to me, Frostvang?" There was a slight tremor in the boy's voice.

"The greatest of the Pandyr and the greatest of the Bearzyrk." Frostvang turned and strode back to his mount.

Frostpaw shouted to the big Bearzyrk, "You're leaving?" The wind whipped up into a fury.

"I will leave you to speak. I will return at dawn with your father and the clans. From here we will all journey to the Aesirmyr!" shouted Frostvang without turning to look back. "Go, Frostpaw. Speak to the fallen. Hear our story."

Frostpaw watched Frostvang climb upon the spearhorn and head back toward the caves. When the old Bearzyrk disappeared into the storm, Frostpaw turned around and went into the Den of the Slayers.

CHAPTER 22

THORGRID AND THE UNDER-KING

ILES BELOW THE RAGING wars in the upper world, the realm of the Under-King was a cold and silent place, a shadowy reflection of the world. There was death in this realm just as there was in the one above. But there was also life, ancient and primitive life. The Under Realm was filled with as much life as the upper realms boasted, if not more. While fields of sun-kissed grass and wind-cooled trees dotted the surface of Mistgard, deep below, one could find miles of sparkling quartz deposits and phosphorescent niter growing in abundance. Twisting corridors and canyons of stone teemed with a million types of life. Insects, reptiles, invertebrates, and other denizens crawled and crept in these earthen halls. Whereas gray-green oceans raged under sky, cold, deep lakes filled the bowels of the Under Realm; Life thrived down in these silent seas as well.

Life was old in the Under Realm, old and silent like its king. The Under-King, Fell, was master of this dark kingdom, and just as Sprign had her children far above, so, too, did the Under-King far below. His underkin worked tirelessly and without complaint in the world beneath the world. Miles of passages were shaped by the underkin beneath the watchful eye of their Under-King. It was said that there were paths that led to every island and mountain in Mistgard.

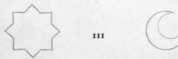

The Under-King had labored for thousands of years to sculpt the ribs and spine of the Under Realm. With but a word and a breath, stone was shaped and crystalline arches spiraled from cavern floors. Around every turn, gardens of quartz, amethyst, and jade sprouted from lichen-coated bedrock, and Fell and his minions dwelled peacefully in this quiet world of antediluvian splendor. But even amidst this primordial beauty, the Under-King grieved.

Brooding and silent, Fell roamed his kingdom. The young Pandyr had been down in the realm for many days and had made do with whatever primal essentials Fell was able to provide. He held no feelings for the whelps, but he provided for them nonetheless; it was what Sprign would have wanted from him.

As he walked the crystal-illuminated paths, he noticed that bits of pine needles and dried petals of some upper-world flora were scattered across the stone floor. A deep rumble echoed from his chest and, in turn, throughout his realm. In an instant, the stone giant's frame melded into the wall and was gone, only to re-form in the room of Sprign's burial mound. His minions would have no desire or need to come to Sprign's resting place. In front of Fell, bits of hay and fallen twigs lay strewn across the floor; the remnants led toward the chambers of the Pandyr cubs.

His anger shook the earth. Fell's form was once again absorbed into the rock, and he disappeared.

***

The earth shook, and Thorgrid hushed a crying cub and tried unsuccessfully to feed another from a cup of milky, mineral-rich water and honey. Thorgrid had the cubs gathered in a large cave, and she ran the children, both older and younger, as her father commanded his warriors. Some made beds while others prepared mushrooms and pounded roots into a mash for supper. Thorgrid's father, Thoryn, would hardly have believed that the headstrong child he had left days ago would be so capable of handling a room full of squalling cubs.

"Calm now; be brave. We are safe here. Once my father and the clans defeat the giants, they will return for us, and we can all be back home, where we will feast and sing and tell stories all night long. You want me to let them know how strong you were, right?" After fumbling around in her sleeping area, Thorgrid handed a mewling tot a small handmade doll. "Here you go," said Thorgrid in a gentle voice. "I know it's not as fine as the ones you have back at Sunspear Hall, but it's all we have here unless you want to snuggle up to some old rock."

"Dolly!" said the young Anji, granddaughter of Byorgn, the Sunspear chieftain. She pulled on the toy roughly, and Thorgrid sternly corrected her.

"You be gentle now! This isn't just a dolly, Anji." Thorgrid carefully straightened the doll's braids. "See here? This is Sprign."

The homemade doll was fashioned from woven grass and dried pine needles bound tightly to form a primitive figurine. Bits of shell and stone were tied to a small dress made out of a torn silk banner. Her hair was shiny green hay, and it was braided and tied with some silver twine plucked from the hem of a cloak. It was crudely crafted but had taken Thorgrid hours to create. The first one she made had been given to a young Darkcloud cub who was lonely for her mother. After that, other cubs had asked for their own Sprign dolls.

"Sprign was the mother of the entire upper world. She is the one who made the animals in the forests and the birds in the sky." The children were quiet while Thorgrid told them the tale. Some mouthed the words silently with her, while others lay down amongst the blankets and watched intently. "She was the one who made the Pandyr, too! She gave us life and made us strong. She gave us the courage to live, and to fight even against—"

"The giants!" Anji blurted out.

"Yes, the giants or anyone else who would try to hurt us," replied Thorgrid in her best grown-up voice. "She—" Thorgrid stopped when she noticed they were not alone.

From out of a stony wall, the Under-King emerged, startling the cubs. "Be at ease, little ones. I was merely listening to your . . . story."

He towered over the cubs; only Thorgrid seemed unafraid of the Under-King. Fell noticed this. There were clearly hints of her father in the way she carried herself. He walked slowly over to them and spoke as softly as a voice born of gravel could speak. "May I see the doll?"

"It's not a dolly. It's Sprign," said young Anji defiantly.

"I see, little Sunspear. May I see Sprign, then?" said the Under-King. Only with great coaxing from Thorgrid did Anji hold out the doll to the giant, who looked at it fondly while he gently turned it around in his large hands.

"Give me back Sprign. She's mine!" little Anji said angrily.

"She is very lovely. Sprign would have been happy with your work, Thorgrid. Please pardon my intrusion." The Under-King returned the doll to its pebble-sized owner and moved to leave.

Thorgrid looked up at the giant and spoke. "Under-King?"

Fell turned and looked down at the Hammerheart cub. Thorgrid seemed a bit hesitant at first, standing toe to toe with the Under-King just as her father had days ago. The fiery will of the Hammerheart urged her on, and she asked her question. "Under-King, did—did you want me to make you one, too?"

The Under-King's face was as impassive as stone. "You want to make me a doll?" he said.

"Only if you want me to," Thorgrid said.

"*It's not a dolly. It is Sprign!*" shouted Anji from her bedroll.

Fell looked at Thorgrid and then nodded. "Yes, yes, I would like that very much," he said.

Thorgrid took up some handfuls of grass and slowly began forming the body. She looked up at the giant, who stood and watched her work. "It, uh, it might take a little time," said Thorgrid.

The Under-King sat his massive body on the stone floor next to the cubs. "Then I will wait," he said softly.

CHAPTER 23

THE HALL OF THE DEAD

HE DEN OF THE SLAYERS WAS cold and still. The walls had been hewn from what looked like ancient glacier ice, and a pale blue glow glimmered across the floor. An old brazier of horn and bone stood on each side of the hallway. Frostpaw struck steel to stone, and the dry wood within lit immediately. He grabbed a length of timber and looked around the den. The walls were covered with weapons and armor of ancient make and design. Tapestries and furs of strange beasts dotted the hallway sporadically, and every so often another brazier would appear, which Frostpaw would bring to life as well. The very air seemed old, and Frostpaw knew that he was the only living thing in this tomb. Still, he felt far from alone.

Along the hallway were thrones and altars upon which rested the bodies of the dead. Some of the deceased were still relatively preserved. Some were clad in great suits of boiled leather and bone armor, with hardly a patch of fur or mane showing. Here and there, thrones were adorned with old drinking horns, pelts, and various other trophies. All of the fallen bore some sort of elaborate scrollwork that hung in curls about their bodies.

Maybe they are the chronicles of the warriors' deeds and history, thought Frostpaw as he worked his way farther down the hallway. He could not read the writings, for they were not in the common language of the Pandyr. The inscriptions looked like a series of scratches and claw marks rather than the runes of the Pandyr tongue.

One odd feeling that Frostpaw had, standing amongst the bodies of the long dead, was that he was not afraid, not in the slightest. He felt a gentle peace and, oddly enough, a sense of belonging. It was the feeling one felt when one returned home after a very long journey. Frostpaw didn't know if that was a good reaction; after all, he was standing in the halls of the time-lost dead.

Frostpaw continued down, deeper and deeper into the Den of the Slayers, until he noted a strange purple light emanating from the end of the hall. It appeared to be coming from behind a great door, silhouetting it with a similar purple glow. He felt such calm that he did not even start when the giant door opened on its own.

The room he entered was round and similar in size to the great hall in Thunder's Home. A large hearth stood in the hall, but the strange light came not from there but from the other end, high atop a set of steps. The room was tiered, consisting of three levels. On the first two tiers sat more thrones, two on the right and two on the left on each level. In the middle of the tiers was a stairway carved into the turquoise ice. It stopped at the third tier, where one solitary throne sat high above all the others. Unlike the other thrones, this one was not made of horn, wood, and stone but was rather carved out of the same blue ice that made up the stairs and the walls. All of the thrones had the remnants of Bearzyrk upon them, but unlike the fallen warriors in the corridor above, these bodies were no more than skin and bone. And one stood out above all.

In the center throne, on the highest seat in the room, sat a humongous Bearzyrk skin curled over a pair of horns. It hung heavily and was so large that it fell to the floor like a massive cloak. The fur was glowing white. Behind the skin, held firmly by a set of twisting elkhorn antlers, rested a large hunting horn and a pair of gigantic spears. It was from the weapons that the violet light emanated. One spearhead was burning blue ice; the other was of crimson flame. Together, the blades created a vibrant purple light that lit the hall with its radiance. Both spearheads seemed to bore into Frostpaw as if they were eyes staring into his mind.

Frostpaw walked up the frozen steps till he was a mere foot from the high seat. There on the throne hung the skin of the mightiest of Bearzyrk. In a trembling voice, Frostpaw spoke. "I have come as you asked."

Though no wind blew in the hall, the skin upon the throne moved. Frostpaw gasped as the skin twisted and formed into the shape of a massive figure. A spectral glow burned in his eyes, and the apparition spoke.

"Frostpaw, I am Ghostmane."

CHAPTER 24

THE GRANDFATHER SPEAKS

FROSTPAW STOOD STARING at the specter amazed but still
unafraid. The figure was a sight to behold. Nine feet tall at the
shoulders and powerful in build. He spoke with a thick accent, but
his words were clear and strong: "I would tell you our story."

Frostpaw listened to what the grandfather of the Bearzyrk
had to say. "It was many years ago when Ghostmane was born. I was once
ruler of the greatest of all the Pandyr clans . . . the noble Sunspear. My father
passed early in his life, and I was made chieftain at a very young age.

"I was called Ironmane for my blackish-blue hair. I was tall and strong,
massive in body and handsome in features. Proud and boastful I was, but I
led the clans against the giants and defended our shores from the beasts of
the great green seas.

"After many years of battle, our lands were free of strife and danger. I had
earned the love of my people and of the other clans as well. The Sunspear
clan shone bright upon the isle of Mistgard, and for generations we led the
Pandyr through a time of great splendor. There was even talk of uniting the
clans. The Den Mother, Sprign, still walked among us back in my time, and
she was to hold a feast honoring a rare birth among the elkhorn king's herd.
It was said that a golden fawn had been born to the king's mate, and we

Sunspear were overjoyed, as the color of the fawn was the same as our clan's banners! The birth of a golden fawn was an omen of good fortune, and we were honored that the king and his herds had chosen our lands as the place for this momentous event. We went in celebration to the open fields where they lived. Normally we would have been greeted by the swiftest of the king's runners."

Ghostmane paused a moment before continuing. "We were not greeted by anything other than a frigid, bone-biting chill. We searched and searched but found nothing . . . The hours passed, and eventually we found them."

Ghostmane's demeanor changed, and the room darkened. "We found them all . . . slaughtered. The entire herd had been killed with a viciousness created by no regular predator. Bodies were bent, and their horns had been broken off from their skulls with such force that it twisted their necks completely around. We knew no mere pack of jaegyr hounds did this. The stink of frost and the mark of Icegard clung to the carcasses."

The air hung heavy in the den as the spirit of Ghostmane pondered the foul deed. "The bodies were frozen. Ice coated their broken forms. Upon further searching, we found the golden fawn. And with the fawn lay his mother and the king, the great elkhorn king. Their deaths were the worst . . ." Frostpaw watched Ghostmane burn with rage. Clearly the memory still haunted his long-dead spirit.

"The murderers of Wintyr had stolen into my land and disgraced our people with this act. Whether it was done out of revenge for our years of thwarting Wintyr, or whether it was a simple act of carnage, I do not know. The birth of the golden fawn was turned from a good omen to a curse. Our land fell barren, and the other clans turned their backs on the Sunspear, unwilling to associate with what they deemed a 'cursed' clan."

Ghostmane's ire rose, and the hate seemed to warm the air in the den. "My anger and arrogance consumed me. I demanded blood for this outrage. I said that I would redeem my clan by avenging the deaths of the elkhorn king and his herd, or I would not return at all. I gathered a group of my finest trackers, and we went to hunt down the murderous invaders. Sprign herself told me not to go. She, the mother of all Pandyr, pleaded with me not to pursue this labor, but I was inconsolable. All I cared about was the insult to my clan's honor and, more important, to my own."

Ghostmane laughed low and sadly. "How much would have changed if I had only listened to our Den Mother." The apparition flickered in the cold air and did not speak, as if reflecting on the past.

After many moments, he continued. "I took my hunters and followed the bloody trail of the murderers to the beaches of Mistgard. On the shores, we saw our ships lay in ruins, hulls were breached and sails were shredded to scraps—only one remained untouched. A mocking laughter drifted off the northern waves, and we turned towards the sound. There, on the horizon, glimmered a lurid blue light, a ghostly beacon that would guide us to our fate. We boarded the last ship and ventured across the great gray sea.

"Our journey was long and plagued with storms and, just when we thought we had lost our trail, the laughter would cut through the air and the phantom light would appear on the horizon, guiding us back on course. After weeks of pursuit, the jagged mountains broke through the storm clouds ahead, and even with land in sight, our prey left grim markings for us to follow. Icebergs boasted frozen elkhorn, and bloated bodies were chum in the icy waters. We eventually landed upon the frigid shores of Icegard. There, it was always cold, even during Sprign's time, and food was scarce. I cared not. My anger kept me warm, and my hate kept my belly full."

Ghostmane's words echoed in the den, and the light of his spears bounced brightly off the icy walls. "It seemed as if we tracked ghosts. Everything was a blur of blue and white. Frozen trees, frozen lakes. Everything was dead. Well, not everything. Eventually we found our prey. Or, should I say, they found us.

"A dreadful song came lilting out of the skeletal wastes to our ears. It made the frigid bite of Icegard seem no more than a breeze, for this did not chill the body but froze the very hearts that pumped within our chests. I was immobilized by the sounds of the ghostly choir. And while my men and I stood paralyzed and helpless, that was when the daughters of Wintyr appeared to us.

"Hoary white, they floated across the snow, singing their cursed songs of beguiling. The words they whispered were enough to drive the strongest of spirit to despair, and their beauty was even more deadly. A malevolent blue glow shone fiercely from their eyes, and they fell upon my men. My trackers were slaughtered horrendously whilst I watched, feeble as a newborn cub. One by one, my kin were slain before my eyes, and newfound rage burned deep inside me.

"Perhaps that was what moved my limbs. Perhaps it was my own arrogance that would not allow me to die by the frost daughters of Icegard.

"My lungs filled with power, and I bellowed a battle cry, drowning out the wicked sisters' song. My limbs moved, slowly at first, but then they surged with brutal strength. My roar broke the spell they were weaving in our heads, and my men, the ones left living, freed themselves from the ice witches' call. We rallied and started hewing them down like dead wheat under steel scythes. They tried to flee, but we were drunk with hate and battle lust. All the anger we had felt these many months of searching was unleashed upon them in a moment of pure, unrestrained butchery. At the end of the battle, only I remained standing. My men lay twisted in death. My battle lust still gnawed at me, and my appetite for revenge was still strong.

"One of the fiend's daughters still lived. She bore mortal wounds, and icy mist seeped from her broken body. I picked up this . . . thing, and her touch froze my hands. I wanted to squeeze the last life out of her. No blade would satisfy the hunger I felt. I wanted the intimacy that only claw and fang could convey.

"I lifted her body till we were face to face, and I stared into those deathly cold eyes. I saw the light dance and start to fade. I wanted to snuff that glow from her skull. My claws wrapped around her delicate neck, and I began to squeeze. It was then that I felt her arms wrap around me in a poisonous embrace. Her head moved forward, and her lips pressed upon mine. With this kiss, her last wretched breath filled my lungs."

A shudder shook the place as if Ghostmane once again tasted those cold, evil lips. "I felt a wave of numbness surge through my body, and I remember falling with the lifeless corpse of Wintyr's daughter upon me. I do not remember blacking out, but I remember waking up, buried in a blanket of snow. How long I lay there, I do not recall. I remember breaking free from her icy embrace and walking in a daze back to the landing site. I pushed my boat out to sea on my own, not realizing the feat till I was almost home. Normally it took five strong clansmen to push our longboats free from the ice. I did this myself, and in a haze of pain.

"Long were the weeks I traveled back to Mistgard. When my ship broke the horizon, the crowds that came to greet me sent up a furious cheer. They roared and clapped when they saw the sail pull ashore, emblazoned with sun and spear, but soon their cheers turned to silence.

"As I walked up to my kin and raised my arm in greeting, I saw what they did: my hand was white, as well as my arm. Looking down, I realized that my entire body had turned a pale white in color. I fell to the ground, weak and weary from the deadly hunt. I was quickly taken into my lodge and attended by the clan's finest healers. Nothing they did could change what had happened to me. Even the magic of Sprign was powerless to aid me. Some thought my fur had turned white from fear, and in a fit of rage, I dashed them senseless for the accusation. Some thought it was the long months in Icegard that changed my coat. It was neither fear nor frost that had changed me. It was something as simple as a kiss."

Frostpaw had been sitting for so long that his body had grown numb. Still, he sat and listened to the greatest tale his young ears had ever heard. So engrossed in the story was he that he failed to feel the cave rumble around him nor the ice that fell from the caverns roof.

"Months passed, and still I was afflicted by this curse. I was consumed by fits of uncontrollable rage, similar to the one I had felt in Icegard. Nothing could quell the desire to kill. I was a madman.

"When the fits were upon me, I would go on long trips out to sea to hunt the giant krakens that harried our ships. I would go deep into the mountains to hunt the beasts and packs of jaegyr hounds that attacked our herds. Nothing could assuage my anger. My clan, my people, suffered for my deeds . . ."

He fell silent for some time, as if steadying himself. "One day, a large group of my kin was speaking of a being called 'Ghostmane.' I approached them and asked of whom they spoke. My clansman said, 'We speak of you, Ghostmane. The greatest of our kind, Ironmane, sailed off to Icegard, never to return. What came back in his stead was not Ironmane, just a ghost that assumed his place. A cursed being, cursed for going into Icegard, and he now has returned the curse upon his own clan. Whereas once Ironmane was kind, Ghostmane is cruel. Whereas Ironmane brought friendship, Ghostmane brings enmity. Ironmane is dead, and we are left with his ghostly shell.'

"A fury gripped me, and I grabbed my own kin by the throat. And through a cloud of blue hate, I heard laughter, not the tempting laughter of the ice witches but the sinister bellow of Wintyr himself! The voice of the king of Icegard was speaking to me . . .

As you've killed my kin, you will forever kill your own! Kill now. Kill for your new king!

"It took all of my strength not to snap my brother's spine. I matched the rage of Wintyr inside me with my own indomitable will. I would not be led like a dog to the kill.

I am Ironmane! No . . . I am Ghostmane, the monster you have created but not the monster you can control!

"I put my kinsman down. I removed the golden circlet that I wore as the leader of the Sunspear, and I gave it to him. My heart was heavy but resolute. 'Find a chieftain worthy of the Sunspear. Forgive me, my brothers and sisters. I know how to rid you of my curse.'

"I left my clan and my home that day, never to return. I roamed to the farthest reaches of Mistgard that my body could carry me to, an area of desolation and quiet far from the lives of my clansmen. I lived alone for years. The first season of Wintyr was grueling. His laughter mocked me, and I wandered deeper and deeper into this abandoned land. I had no lodge, so I made my home in a large cave.

"One day, after hours of scouring the lands for food, I wandered back to my cave and found a small bundle within the opening. I approached cautiously and prodded the bundle with my spear. Out of it poured dried fruits and nuts, gourds of milk, honey, and mead, along with hard loaves of bread. I fell to these as a ravenous hound would a kill. That day I feasted better than I had in my entire life. It was also then that I realized I was not alone. I looked up, and it appeared that with the offerings of food had come the clan brother whom I had almost killed in my madness. He said simple words to me that I will never forget.

"'Ironmane was a great ruler, but he was proud and arrogant. Ghostmane was cruel and hateful, but he gave up all he had for the good of his clan. We will not forget either of you.'

"With those words, he left. And from then on, when Wintyr's rage blew across the lands and Mistgard was frozen in his grip, I would find tributes laid at the opening of my den. One day, I found not only food and drink, but two small cubs waiting for me. It seemed that taking the curse away with me didn't completely free the clans from Wintyr's grasp.

"The cubs were quite young and full of anger and wrath. In the frozen land of the Tundyr, you must quickly learn to master yourself and your environment. Soon they learned to control the violent rages that consumed our kind. The offerings went on for hundreds of seasons, it seemed: food and cloth in Wintyr's time, and mead and honey in Sprign's.

"But eventually, the tributes started to fade away. As the older generations passed on, so did their traditions. As the younger clansmen rose to positions of leadership, they either forgot about us or no longer cared.

"In time, I had forgotten much of my old life as well. I had my own clan again, and our bond was much closer than the one most of the Pandyr shared. We were bonded in life and death. Our bond meant our survival. Without the offerings, we were truly on our own. We had to learn to do many things to survive, things that the more civilized of Mistgard's children would have forsaken. We learned how to hunt beasts and eat their flesh. We wore their furs to stay warm. We became master to all the beasts of the Tundyr. We did what was needed to stay alive, and we made the ultimate sacrifice for our clans . . . We left them."

A rumble shook the cave, but this time it was not from within. This was the slow, distant rumble of thousands of heavy feet charging across the land above. Giant slabs of ice fell from the ceiling to crash upon the thrones and floor. A chunk smashed Frostpaw on his head, and he tumbled down the stairs to land at the bottom in a heap. Dazed, he lifted his eyes. The light of the twin spears was like a beacon calling him home.

"The giants are here," said Ghostmane. "Frostpaw, it is you who will lead our kind against the giants one last time. Pandyr and Bearzyrk."

Frostpaw crawled up to his knees. Pain throbbed in his head. The world was blackening quickly, and the cold was closing in on him. Still, he climbed. All he could see was the red and blue glow of the spears. They looked like scarlet and cobalt eyes burning in his fading consciousness. He reached up to the spears, and just before he touched their hafts, Ghostmane's distant words seeped into his mind.

"Frostpaw . . . make me live once more . . ."

Frostpaw's hands grasped the spears, and he fell into darkness.

CHAPTER 25

BROKEN BOW AND SHATTERED SPEAR

HE CRUDE FIGURINE OF SPRIGN sat motionless upon a small rock. Far within the Under Realm, Fell sat motionless as well, quietly listening to the world tremble. He felt the fear and the confusion of the upper world through every pebble and stone upon the surface. He felt the panic of the beasts and birds. He also felt the horror of the Pandyr. They were above in the upper world, facing the terrible wrath of his brothers.

Too proud to hide in safety, they marched to annihilation. They would rather die free than live in a stone grave. He picked up the tiny doll, straightened its braided straw hair, moved over to Sprign's cairn, and placed the figure atop the mound. "The Pandyr chose a hard life amongst the world rather than the solace and safety of the shadows. They are truly your children, my sister."

The doll fell over, and he positioned a simple gray rock next to it to stabilize it. He reflected on this action for a moment before he melded into the stony wall.

"They are your children, and as you would stand with them, so, too, shall I." The Under-King passed through the walls of the Under Realm, followed by his army of underkin.

***

"Frostpaw?" The Storm Speaker's eyes blinked open. "Where is Frostpaw?"

A large paw patted the shoulder of the old Pandyr. "It is all right, Dark Beard," said Frostvang. "The lad is with an old friend. Come, we must raise the clans and go meet him. From there, we march up the Aesirmyr."

It was still an hour before dawn would change the black clouds to a dull orange-gray. Thunder rumbled across the sky and also seemed to run through the very ground. This bothered the Storm Speaker greatly. He shook the thick blankets from his shoulders and took up his spear. Silently he stood at the mouth of the cave, closed his eyes, and slowly opened his right one. It blazed with a frosty white light, and the Storm Speaker saw through the eyes of the albatross Fog.

Across the frozen lakes marched the armies of the giants. Thousands upon thousands, they surged over the land. Though they were many miles away, the ground beneath the Storm Speaker shook tremulously under the giants' march. He wasted no more time. "Arise, Pandyr! The giants march upon us! We must make it to the Aesirmyr before they arrive. Mount up and ride."

Shouts echoed through the caves as the Pandyr chaotically readied for their escape. Just then, Gloam floated in and landed on the Storm Speaker's shoulder, chirping frantically in his ear. The Storm Speaker started and whispered, "Sprign bless us!"

The Hammerheart chieftain came up swiftly, followed by some of his clansmen and several Jadebow. "What is it, Storm Speaker? Are the giants upon us?" Thoryn had his hammer out and was eager to put it to use.

"Not yet, but we must move swiftly. The Sunspear return."

Thoryn steadied himself before he spoke. "And Ullyr and his men? Do they return with them?"

The Storm Speaker looked grimly at the chieftain. "Yes, Thoryn, they return . . . what is left of them." The Jadebow clansmen gave each other worried glances as the Storm Speaker closed his eyes and reached out with his senses. "I feel Ullyr's mind calling out. He still lives, but his life fades by the second. Make haste, Hammerheart. Ride to meet them."

"Father!"

As Thoryn and his riders went forth into the dawning day, the Storm Speaker turned to catch a frantic Ursara. Her eyes darted around wildly as tears started to form. "Father, Frostpaw is gone." He took her into his arms and comforted her as best as he could.

Frostvang put a hand on her as well. "Easy, lass. Frostpaw is not missing. He went with me to a place our kind reveres. He is safe; we will ride to him and go to the Aesirmyr."

The Storm Speaker's face told otherwise. "The Den of the Slayers is gone, Frostvang."

The large bear looked at him steadily. "What? How do—"

"Through Fog. While he soared above, I saw what was left of it. The den lay in ruins, smashed in the wake of the giants' path."

"No!" cried Ursara as she lunged past the two elders and made her way to the opening of the cave. She was right at the mouth when she stopped in midstride.

From out of the storm came what was left of the shattered Sunspear clan. Some staggered in on their own, while the Hammerheart and the Jadebow aided those too badly wounded to do it alone. As his clansmen moved by with the Sunspear, Thoryn called out for the Jadebow chieftain. "Ullyr! By Sprign, come forth, you old war dog!"

There was no answer for many moments, until a lone voice was heard coming in from the storm. "Red beard, over here!"

Thoryn looked through the sleet as the great figure of Ullstag emerged from the storm at the cave's mouth. He was bruised and burned but not broken. Upon his shoulders, he carried what Thoryn sought.

"Ullyr!" Thoryn rushed over to Ullstag and helped him carry the wounded Jadebow chieftain to a blanketed area of the cave. Ullyr was near death. His right arm was mangled, and his face was awash with blood that poured from a ruined eye socket.

Thoryn laid the Jadebow chief upon the rough-spun covers and noticed that Ullstag had carried more than Ullyr. Across his shoulders rested Ullyr's mount, Dawnstrider.

The elkhorn's body was still.

Ullyr was shivering and shaking all over, frozen to the core. "My men . . . my—Dawnstrider . . . where—"

Thoryn looked around uneasily, unsure of what to say to the grieving chieftain. "Easy, friend. We have Dawnstrider; she is here. You need to rest now." Thoryn's words seemed to calm the chieftain as he slipped into unconsciousness.

The ground no longer rumbled but shook furiously. The Pandyr were in a panic. Futilely, the Storm Speaker tried to create some kind of order out of the chaos. "Pandyr, listen to me!" he said frantically. "The giants have made their way to the caves. There is no other alternative but to stand and fight. Thoryn, I leave it to you and your Hammerheart to make the first line of defense."

"Aye, Storm Speaker!" shouted the Hammerheart chieftain.

In the distance, howls came from the incoming host. The roars of the giants of Firehome and Icegard filled the cavern with dread. Strangely, it was no longer just the ground that shook. The entire cave seemed to move, but the greatest upheaval was in the back. Two large arms appeared out of the rocky surface and dug fingers of stone into the very wall of the cave. With effortless force, the arms opened up a gaping hole that led deep into the earth. A path loomed in the opening, lit with numerous glowing crystals of topaz and amethyst.

Fell's graveled baritone echoed throughout the cave. "Run, Pandyr. Be swift. My brothers approach."

The Storm Speaker quickly found his tongue. "Come now! Hurry to me. We go into the Under Realm."

The Pandyr, startled at first, hurried into the gaping hole; better to face what lay in the darkness than to confront the howling fury of the giant hordes. The Hammerheart chieftain and his clansmen helped get the wounded Sunspear and the fallen Jadebow chieftain into litters and then swept them down into the depths. All who remained were the Storm Speaker, Ursara, and Frostvang.

Ursara was wild with fear. "I'm not leaving without Frostpaw, Father!"

The Storm Speaker took her by the shoulders and pleaded with his daughter. "There is nothing we can do about Frostpaw now. We must flee, or we will die here."

Ursara was about to protest, but both she and the Storm Speaker were lifted bodily and thrust into the cave mouth by Frostvang. "Go now! I will find Frostpaw and bring him back. I promise you, Dark Beard's daughter."

Ursara was hesitant, but the Storm Speaker was finally able to persuade her. "Ursara, I can feel the life of Frostpaw; even miles away, it burns with a power I have never felt before. For now, he is safe. But if he were indeed gone, then know this: He would want you to live."

The Bearzyrk touched the Storm Speaker's shoulder firmly. "Dark Beard, I will bring him back to you . . . to all of you. Go, now!"

The Storm Speaker looked at his friend. "Please, Frostvang . . . find my son."

The Bearzyrk nodded briskly and ran into the storm. Just as his shape vanished in the frigid mist, the arms pushed the rock wall together again, and the mouth of the cave sealed up, blocking the tide of blue and red giantkin as they slammed against the rocky surface, futilely pummeling the thick stone. Above the fray, the mountain shook, and a wave of rolling death pounded down upon the giantkin then, crushing them beneath a landslide of punishing rock.

Through the dust clouds and the groans of the fallen emerged a gigantic figure of living fire. A giant sword of burning iron hammered the mountain but did no more than scratch it. Fiery words came forth and were soon lost in the howl of the wind.

"Brother . . . you will pay."

CHAPTER 26
A GHOST IN THE RUINS

FROSTVANG THUNDERED ACROSS the Tundyr on his spearhorn. He blazed through frost bursts and clouds of fire and pushed his harried beast for all that it had. As he neared the Den of the Slayers, his words caught in his throat. "No, no, no . . ."

He leapt from his mount and crashed into the ground. Then he rolled and ran to the ruins. The Den of the Slayers lay smashed upon the earth, a broken mound of splintered ice. He heaved with all his might, but even the Bearzyrk's great strength could not manage to move the doorway of stone and ice. His fists pounded against the slab.

"Frostpaw! Answer me, boy!"

Steam came out of Frostvang's maw in gusts. In the wake of the giants, the air was ablaze with whorls of ash and frost. The great Bearzyrk heaved again, but his efforts proved useless. The sound of ice crunching under heavy feet brought him out of his frenzy, and he whirled, spear in hand.

From out of the gust came the large, bulky shapes of the Bearzyrk clan. Frostvang lowered his spear, pleading. "Brothers, help me. The lad is trapped below. The giants—"

"The giants were not our concern," said Grymir caustically. "Had you let it be, the giants would not have even been within our lands. They would

135

have crushed the Pandyr and been done with it. It is you who has brought the giants' wrath upon our clan."

"You are a fool to believe that, Grymir! The giants will not stop until all of their enemies are crushed, including the Bearzyrk. Are we not the kinsmen of Ghostmane? Sumyr and Wintyr both lust for revenge for the pain Ghostmane brought to them so many years before. You think cowering in a cave will save your worthless hide?"

The elder Bearzyrk struck Frostvang with a speed that belied his age. Frostvang barely managed to throw up his arm in defense before he was smashed by Grymir's spear haft. He tried to rise but was knocked down again, this time held fast under the crushing weight of Grymir's clawed foot. "You will suffer for your deeds. You've desecrated the most sacred place in our realm, and for what? To aid the likes of the Pandyr?"

"We—we are Pandyr!" Frostvang pleaded. "If we stand together again, we may have a chance of—"

"Wrong, traitor! You sided with our enemy, and look what's happened . . . You've brought the wrath of the giants upon us!" The old bear raised his spear, and its horned tip hung menacingly over Frostvang's neck. With a shriek, Grymir brought the weapon down.

A shock shifted the earth beneath the Bearzyrk, and Frostvang grabbed Grymir's foot, wrenching it away. Grymir howled, and his horned spear crashed down on empty snow as Frostvang rolled to the side. The ground shook again, and the mound of ice and stone moved. The sound of heavy footsteps echoed in the air, but the tread came not from outside but from deep within the ruins. A faint light emanated from inside the collapsed den.

The Bearzyrk looked at each other grimly as Grymir screamed at Frostvang. "It's a trap! The giants hide below in our most sacred place. You have doomed us, Frostvang!"

Grymir shouted commands as the footsteps grew louder and closer. "Bearzyrk, the giants march from below! Be ready to attack!"

Massive ice sheets rose and crashed to the ground. A haunting purple light emanated from the opening, and a powerful form emerged whose silhouette dwarfed the gathered Bearzyrk. They stumbled back, shocked at what they saw. Even Grymir froze at the shape that moved toward him. The figure strode ahead and looked at the clansmen. The eyes that blazed in front of them were the color of icy blue fire. The figure raised his arms into the burning sky, and in each of his clawed white fists was a spear: one of fire and one of ice.

Grymir backed away slowly, shaking his matted mane. "No, it cannot be."

The figure spoke. "Your poisoned words are done . . . They corrupt the minds and hearts of those you were trusted to lead. You will lead no more."

"You cannot be! You—you are dead . . . You can't be—"

Frostvang stood up and motioned for the crowd to gather near.

"For many hundreds of years, you have been forbidden to go to the Den of the Slayers, forbidden to know our story. Now you will know; you will know everything." The figure looked at the clansmen as a father would his children. "My brothers, it was many years ago when Ghostmane was born . . ."

***

The Bearzyrk listened quietly. Though they were pelted by ice and fire, their attention was given to naught but Ghostmane, for they knew that the

words he spoke were true. When Ghostmane finished, he silently looked over the crowd.

Grymir sputtered furiously. "No, do not listen to these words. The Pandyr cast us out and left us to die. We owe them nothing!"

Ghostmane looked at the twisted old bear in sadness. "I fear some will never learn. I was not banished by the Pandyr. I left the Pandyr out of love for my clan. Out of my love for all the clans! Now the clans have need of me again. Will I forsake them in the direst of times?" Ghostmane gazed sternly at the Bearzyrk. "Will you forsake them all over ancient feuds and time-lost grudges?"

Frostvang spoke first. "I will stand with the Pandyr. I will fight for Mistgard. Brothers, will you join me?" He looked over at Grymir in disgust. "Or will you cower in hate?"

Several of the Bearzyrk walked over to Frostvang and offered their arms in union. Over the next few moments, more of the Bearzyrk moved to Frostvang's group, until only Grymir and his wolves stood outside the circle.

Frostvang turned from his brothers and looked at the ancient one with pity.

"Will you not join with us, Grymir? We are your family still. Hearts can change; they must simply be allowed to."

Grymir stared at Frostvang with a deadly eye.

Frostvang shook his head and turned toward the other Bearzyrk. "Brothers, we will start for the Aesirmyr—"

A guttural scream split the dawn air, and Grymir hurtled forward, wolves at his side and his spear held high. "Fools, you doom us all! This is naught but children's stories and lies!"

Frostvang leapt to the side but slipped on the iced earth. The spear of Grymir arced down toward the prostrate Frostvang in a killing stroke, but it never landed. Instead of flesh and fur, it met with fire and ice.

Startled out of his charge, Grymir looked up to see the massive shape of Ghostmane looming before him, spears crossed, blocking his strike. The wolves cowered away from the First of the Bearzyrk's stare.

"As you banished the Pandyr, so do I banish you from the Bearzyrk. Go now, and live. If you stay . . ." Ghostmane twisted his spears together, snapping Grymir's spear in two. Its haft fell to the snow; the top half went whirling into the fog.

Grymir looked at the crowd and slowly backed up, then turned to disappear into the mist, wolves howling at his heels. "Fools . . . you will all pay for this."

The Bearzyrk stood silent in the freezing morning mist. Frostvang gathered his mount and offered it to Ghostmane. Ghostmane shook his head. From his back he drew forth a large hunting horn, and he raised it to his bearded lips. The strength of the horn's blast cleared the clouds above, momentarily letting the sun shine warmly upon the Bearzyrk before it was once again swallowed by the storm.

A thundering sound rolled across the Tundyr, and from out of the fog ran a herd of spearhorn unlike any the Bearzyrk had ever seen. They charged upon the surface of the frozen lake at a full gallop and stopped at the raised hand of Ghostmane. From out of the herd emerged a gigantic spearhorn that dwarfed its fellows by many hands. Ghostmane walked up to the great beast and leapt upon its back. Its matted coat, like those of the entire herd, was as white as the frost they trod upon.

"To the Aesirmyr we ride."

In a second, Ghostmane disappeared into the mist.

The remaining spearhorn walked over to the Bearzyrk and stood, waiting. Frostvang looked at his clan and, with a shrug, mounted a white spearhorn. With a great burst of speed, he and the spearhorn vanished into the fog, soon to be followed by the entire clan of Bearzyrk. In a few heartbeats, all were gone from sight, swallowed by the morning mists.

The last to leave the Tundyr was a small black bird that flew frantically toward the Aesirmyr Peaks.

CHAPTER 27

IN THE HALLS OF
THE UNDER-KING

THE STORM SPEAKER AND THE clans traveled wearily into the depths of the Under Realm. The path before them was a twisting series of narrow ledges that climbed ever upward to the earthen rafters of the mountain. Though steep in design, the road was free of the debris and rubble usually associated with underground paths. The normally dark world was lit by an ever-changing array of phosphorescent moss and glowing shards of crystal. Though their pace was furious, there were times of rest while the Pandyr traveled upon gigantic earthen slabs. Huge blocks of moving rock carried the weary clansmen hundreds of feet into the air or across great estuaries, dropping them off at yet another pathway that climbed ever upward.

Mog'aw, the Thundermaw chieftain, marveled at the craftsmanship and design of the shifting bridges and massive stone lifts. He rubbed his hand over the stone appreciatively. "Impressive. I cannot see a single chisel mark," he said with admiration. The Thundermaw were renowned builders of Mistgard's greatest hearths and lodges.

"These halls were formed not by tools but by the will of the Under-King," said the Storm Speaker. "He needs only to wish them to be as his mind sees

them, and it is done. The greatest masons of our clans could only dream of possessing such skills."

The Thundermaw chieftain gave a dismissive grunt at the Storm Speaker's words, but he could hardly argue with their truth.

Ursara had been in tear-filled silence since first departing into the Under Realm. The Storm Speaker gave her what solace he could, but nothing he could say would bring her out of her spell. He even tried looking through the eyes of Fog, but to no avail. Try as he might to catch a glimpse of where Frostpaw was, he found that his powers were useless within the Under-King's realm.

"Frostvang will return with Frostpaw, Daughter. He knows our destination and will find us."

Ursara held the small heart-shaped charm that Frostpaw had made for her.

The journey through the labyrinthine caves was difficult on all the senses. The utter silence and the absence of sky, wind, and rain made the Pandyr feel as if they were in a tomb, especially the Iceclaw and Ironbeard clansmen, as sea-roving mariners were unused to such claustrophobic surroundings.

"I'd gladly face the giants above just to get out of this cavernous coffin," said Ur'sog of the Iceclaw.

Tyr'og of the Ironbeard clearly felt the same, though he kept his tongue silent.

"Be patient, little ice chieftain," rumbled the deep voice of Fell. "You are near the end of your journey. Soon you will have more open sky than you can possibly imagine. And giants as well."

The only clan seemingly unaffected by the subterranean world was the Darkcloud. The Darkcloud clansmen were Mistgard's greatest artisans, and they dwelled within a series of connecting caves and passages that were decorated with pictograms of their clan's history. Even in these dire times, the gloomy leader of the Darkcloud, Modyr, rejected the brief respites and, with gouache and brush, painted images on the Under-King's walls. Whether he did it to mark their passage for a possible return or to tell of the clans' final hours, none knew.

After many hours, the twisting path ended straight into a cavern wall, and the Pandyr came to a halt, thankful for the moment's rest. All too suddenly, the wall opened with a splitting sound, followed by a dazzling beam of golden light. The cave lit up with a million sparkling points as the crystal-flecked walls blossomed into a shimmering array of dazzling colors. The Pandyr

MOGÁU

MODYR

were momentarily blinded by the illumination. After their eyes adjusted, the Pandyr walked out of the cave and stood at their destination—atop the Aesirmyr Peaks.

Far above them, to the east, was the golden skull, while to the west floated the ghostly silver skull. The Skulls in the Sky hung calmly, while many miles below them roared the black and burning storm clouds. From their perch, the Pandyr looked down upon the storms of Wintyr. Truly it felt as if they were atop the world, safe from the storms, and that added some steel to the Pandyr's disposition.

"Come, my friends. We haven't much time," said the Storm Speaker.

The clan leaders walked the perimeter and began laying out battle plans while their clansmen erected tents and shelters for the wounded and started prepping their defenses. Ullstag stood watch outside the tent in which Ullyr rested. The other Jadebow clansmen readied arrows and tended to their mounts, grooming and watering them. All of the clans, from the Mistcloak to the few remaining Sunspear, were bursting with newfound hope and purpose.

The only one who was not busy with duties was the Storm Speaker. He stood silent and still as he gazed out at the everlasting ocean of clouds below him and the brilliant, cloudless sky above.

The skulls move together, thought the Storm Speaker sadly. *At the creation of the world, the skulls came together and made the giants. Now it appears that they will come together for the end as well.*

Atop the Aesirmyr, the Pandyr clans of Mistgard readied themselves for their final battle. There was an air of determination and fierceness in their demeanor. The Thundermaw chieftain and his clansmen were lacking any sadness. They relished the hard labor, constructing fortifications and breathing in the clean air. Mog'aw and his Thundermaw moved giant boulders with burly arms, stacking them into crude but sturdy walls and battlements.

The Under-King silently watched the clansmen until Mog'aw spoke up in irritation. "You think you can lend us a hand with all this rock work? You are a master at this, or so I've been told," he jeered at the Under-King.

The Under-King beckoned for the Thundermaw to move aside, and then he spread his arms wide. "Awaken," he said in a booming voice, and the rock barriers that the Thundermaw had created crumbled and were re-formed into a jagged bulwark, complete with arrow slits and sharp crystal shards jutting from the top.

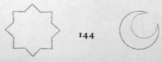

The Thundermaw clansmen bristled, but old Mog'aw burst out laughing and clapped the Under-King on his rocky side. "Excellent work. Now, if only you could make about a dozen more here, here, and here," he said, pointing at various strategic positions all around the base camp.

The Under-King looked down at the Thundermaw chieftain, clearly disliking that he'd been tricked into his service. But soon, his frown broke and turned into what might be considered a smirk. With a rumble, Fell proceeded to summon protective walls where Mog'aw had so kindly asked him to. When finished, Fell nodded in satisfaction, dusting the rock powder from his hands.

Near the center of the camp, Ullstag entered the tent set up for the wounded. He bore a bundle wrapped in his worn cloak. He passed Ullyr's pack of hounds, and they looked up at the Bearzyrk with bloodshot eyes; they, too, mourned for their master. Ullstag saw Ullyr, and his great heart grew heavy.

Ullyr was lying at the back of the tent, resting as best as one could in such a condition. The Jadebow chieftain had lost much from bringing back the Sunspear. His left eye was gone, the socket covered by a crude cloth wrap. His right arm was missing at the shoulder, and his right leg was braced in a heavy splint.

"Your wounds are serious but appear to be on the mend," said Ullstag.

"I'll live another day, it seems. Would that Dawnstrider could be here, too, so we could make our final charge together."

Ullstag nodded grimly. He knew the feeling well. At his heart, Ullstag was still a Jadebow clansman, and the Jadebow had a special affinity with their mounts. From what he could gather, Ullyr had helped bring his golden elkhorn, Dawnstrider, into the world and had trained her from her first steps.

"Your final charge need not be alone," said Ullstag. He placed the bundle he carried onto the bed, careful not to bump into Ullyr's broken limb.

Ullyr looked at the package with his remaining eye, then looked at the old bear. Ullstag nodded, motioning for the chieftain to open it. Ullyr pulled back the cloak, and underneath glistened golden fur. He gazed at the Bearzyrk in shock. "Is this Da—?" he said, shaking his head.

"Aye, Chieftain. You would not leave her even as her body pulled you down into the depths. I had no choice but to bring you both back." The golden pelt gleamed in the twilight, casting glints of amber onto the tent's canvas walls. "She died on our trek back from the lake. I could not let her die alone, nor could I leave her to the giants. She deserved a better end. But she can still finish writing her saga in the final battle."

The Bearzyrk moved aside the pelt, and Ullyr's shocked expression turned to one of horror. Under the fur wrap lay a set of golden antlers. They were expertly bound together at the base, and at their farthest tips, they were connected by a taut piece of sinew.

"Dawnstrider." Ullyr breathed deeply as a tear rolled down his right cheek.

"Dawnstrider has passed, but still she will live on." The Bearzyrk placed a large quiver of arrows next to the bundle. Their make was crude and unremarkable with the exception of the tips. The arrowheads were made of smooth golden horn. "What you hold is Dawnstrider's revenge, and it is this that will be with you in the final fight against the giants. She will avenge the wrong done to her, and to her master. Her funeral hymn will be sung at dawn tomorrow, and her voice will sing a deadly chorus to the enemy."

The old bear left Ullyr to ponder the gift, but before he closed the tent flap, he spoke softly. "I know this is not your way, little chieftain. I do not know your customs for honoring your dead. This is our way, and it is how I honored my own when he passed. I could think of no better way to honor Dawnstrider."

Ullstag let the tent flap close behind him. Ullyr whispered something that was lost to the Bearzyrk. Looking back, he saw a subtle glow from within the tent; the light came from the bow made of elkhorn antlers. Ullyr spoke again, this time with more conviction. This time, Ullstag did not fail to hear what was spoken.

"Dawn Breaker."

CHAPTER 28

ALL THE CHILDREN
OF MISTGARD

TENSIONS WERE HIGH AMONG THE CLANS of Mistgard. The giants were coming, but for now, the hour was silent and stark. The Pandyr took shifts watching the perimeter, and the ones not on duty took time to mend armor or even tried to get a few moments' rest.

The Storm Speaker sat atop the highest peak, watching with his other eyes. He stood up stiffly, and from below the cloud cover, horns blared and bleated out discordant sounds. The great albatross, Fog, rose slowly through the clouds and landed near the Storm Speaker. The bird was streaked from smoke, and his feathers had been blackened by flame. Atop his back lay Gloam, holding on weakly with his beak. The Storm Speaker took Gloam and spoke softly to him; the little bird clung tenuously to life.

"Ursara, tend to our friend here," he said.

Seeing Gloam in such a state stirred her out of her silence. "The fighting is done for you, little wing. You will rest now," she said as gently as if speaking to her own kin. She walked to her tent and tended to the small black bird with caring hands.

The Storm Speaker smiled, happy to see his daughter's mind focusing on something other than the absent Frostpaw. He was saddened over the

misfortune he had caused Gloam. He had sent the tiny bird and Fog to see if they could glimpse any sign of Frostpaw. Neither Gloam nor Fog had seen the boy.

"Storm Speaker, you should see this!" shouted Thoryn.

Trusting Ursara to care for their little friend, the Storm Speaker stepped down from his watch and moved over to the Hammerheart's side. "The giants?" he asked.

"It is not the giants. But look there, through the clouds. Something approaches . . . and a lot of something, by the size of the group."

Shadows moved slowly through the curtain of storm clouds, and from the mists came the orphans of Mistgard.

Flocks of gray gulls and dusky blackbirds descended, followed by singular or paired storm eagles, mist owls, and sun hawks. Wild elkhorn leapt through the clouds, and from behind them stalked large packs of jaegyr hounds, all covered with ash and frost. Every manner of beast walked through the camp. Small cliff leopards were side by side with horned hares and frost foxes. All of the island's fauna, normally predator and prey to each other, marched together in hopes of finding sanctuary from the wrath the giants had brought to Mistgard. The Pandyr stood amazed at the menagerie. The animals hesitated at the gathering before them, all but one. A grizzled jaegyr hound approached the Storm Speaker, who, upon seeing the beast, smiled at his old acquaintance.

"By Sprign, after all these years," he said as he held out his hand to the big hound. Fenryr's scarred face looked at the Storm Speaker with a bright eye. His other eye was missing, lost in a fight long ago to a cub protecting his herd. "It's good to have you and your pack with us today."

The Storm Speaker and the other Pandyr walked among the animals, letting them sniff and smell them. The Pandyr petted them in return, showing that they were all together in these final hours.

The Under-King stood stoically, watching the horizon. The Storm Speaker saw the look Fell bore, and he knew that the end was drawing near. He spoke strong and powerful words to his kin, both Pandyr and animal. "We are all that are left, my friends, the last of the children of Sprign. From elkhorn, hare, and hound to the eight clans of the Pandyr, we will fight or fall together."

As if in answer, a clamor of horns echoed up through the clouds.

The Storm Speaker looked around the camp one last time. Though his words were bold, his heart felt empty. Without the strength of the Bearzyrk, the final battle seemed doomed. A firm hand gripped him, and he looked down upon the stout Hammerheart chieftain, who grinned savagely.

"Till the last hammer stops singing, there is still a chance," said Thoryn.

"You know, Thoryn, even though I know better, I almost believe you," said the Storm Speaker.

"I almost believe it, too," said Thoryn, laughing softly. The Storm Speaker and the Hammerheart chieftain shook hands and joined the other Pandyr.

Thoryn and his Hammerheart, along with Ullstag and the Jadebow, readied their weapons. Mistcloak and Darkcloud were in position. The Iceclaw, Ironbeard, and Thundermaw, along with what remained of the Sunspear, stood fast. All the clansmen were ready and looking at the Storm Speaker. He raised his spear to them, and they in turn raised their weapons high. The howls of the giants broke the cloud cover, and frost-covered feet and fiery-spurred heels struck the ground. Above the din rose the voices of the Pandyr in unison.

"By tooth and by claw, by fang and by paw!"

The beasts of Mistgard howled, brayed, mewled, and screeched loudly in their tongues as well.

The Pandyr looked toward the parting clouds below them with anticipation and dread. They stood at the top of the world and gazed down upon their doom with fierce eyes and heavy hearts. Surrounding their camp, the armies of the giants approached. These were not mere giantkin. These were the foulest sons of Firehome and Icegard that the brothers commanded. They were tremendous beings of hate and despair, towering as tall as the trees some twenty-five feet in the air. The twisted giantkin that milled around them seemed insignificant compared to the titans of frost and fire. Blades clanged on shields, and as one, the giants surged forward. The world trembled.

At the charge of the enemy, a familiar whirring sound came from the Hammerheart clan. Today, their hammers hummed a funeral dirge, but for whom, it was not yet known. The strain of yew bows sounded behind the thrumming hammers. Thoryn and Ullstag stood side by side, Pandyr and Bearzyrk, brothers of battle. Thoryn's hammer was a whirlwind, and Ullstag's voice a thunderclap.

"Jadebow . . . fire!" boomed the Bearzyrk. A torrent of steel and feathers rained down upon blue and red skin, piercing each color with equal prejudice. Hundreds fell, only to be replaced with a thousand more. The gap was closing, and while the Jadebow reloaded, the Hammerheart advanced.

Thoryn and his clansmen launched their screaming hammers in unison, and the thunderous chorus was followed by bone-crunching thuds and the sound of giants striking earth. Hammers soared back to their masters' hands in time to meet the next wave of the giants' charge.

"Fire at will!" yelled Ullstag, and he began launching his spear-sized arrows into the fray.

Thoryn led his Hammerheart into battle, and the rest of the clans charged with him. The battlements broke the assault of the giants, and they were impaled by spear, lance, and crystal shard. A series of explosive reports echoed across the battlefield as the giants stumbled upon the Mistcloak's tripwires, sending lethal blossoms of sharpened steel twisting through the air.

Fell and his minions moved through the giants like an avalanche. The Under-King shifted his form to a flowing slab of stone and crashed down upon giant flesh, pulverizing it to blue powder and red ash.

Even the animals, though weak and weary, tore into the giants with the primal fury of the wild. Claw and fang stood with horn and hoof, wounding with equal enmity. Beak and talon darted and gouged. The entire island of Mistgard stood united against the foul armies of frost and fire.

Devastation was rampant on the mountain, but it was nothing compared to the wrath of the Storm Speaker. Even the stoic Under-King was surprised at the power of the Oldest of Cubs. At the back of the Pandyr's armies, high atop the tallest of Fell's battlements, stood the lone figure of the Storm Speaker. He called forth and charmed the very storms from the clouds beneath him and sent electric green-and-blue arcs of lightning into the giants' lines, blasting hundreds of their bodies off of the battlefield and into the mist below.

The world above burned. The radiant morning light was blackened by acrid smoke, making the golden skull radiate a brown and bloody glow. The Aesirmyr lay strewn with broken bodies: blue and red intertwined with black and white. Death was not prejudiced on this morning, and she called many to her court.

Still the giants marched, and their screams of pain turned to roars of triumph when their kings entered the fray.

CHAPTER 29

THE CLASH OF THE KINGS

HE BATTLEFIELD SEEMED TO QUIET when his shadow broke the clouds. The air seemed to thicken, and even the light of the Skulls in the Sky seemed to pale. For the first time, the clans of Mistgard were introduced to their own doom. The Bringer of the End walked on the top of the world. Lord Wintyr, ruler of Icegard, entered from the north.

Lord Wintyr stood seventy feet tall and was as massive as a mountain, a living, breathing nightmare of frost and fury. Surrounding him were ripping storms, and wherever he walked, he left a frozen wasteland. His azure skin was covered in jagged ice shards, some of which jutted out chaotically from his shoulders and back. His beard, which hung to his waist, was a vicious array of razor-sharp icicles. His lone eye gleamed; a cold blue light emanated from under his icy helm.

The giantkin's cheers abruptly stopped and turned to screams as they frantically scattered out of Wintyr's path. Those who were too slow were crushed by his heavy stride or frozen solid as he passed them. Upon the battlements and those defending them, he unleashed his fury. Lord Wintyr raised his axe of ice and swung it down to the earth, crushing both battlements and Pandyr equally.

The air became humid, and the ice that coated the earth began to melt and turn the top of the world into a boiling, muddy mess. A howl went up from the giants as the lord of Firehome entered the battlefield from the south.

Clad in black iron and brass ring mail were King Sumyr and his elite guard. Pandyr and beast were mercilessly swept aside by the horrendous fiery arcs of King Sumyr's flaming blade. It cut earth and fur alike, killing and cauterizing in the same instant.

His burning crown of iron blazed above his brow, and the king of Firehome looked for his earthen brother with molten hate. "Where are you, Brother? It's time to pay for your betrayal."

The earth shook, and in a flash, the Under-King rose from the ground beneath Sumyr's feet, toppling the Fire King. Fell clapped his hands together, and a massive dome of rock enveloped Sumyr and crashed down, completely covering him.

A moment later the stones began to glow dully with a fiery light from within. The dome started to shake as King Sumyr rose from the heap, stone liquefying into slag and pooling to the earth. With a roar, Sumyr belched forth a column of crimson fire that consumed the Under-King, whose earthen skin blackened and melted, and the Under-King dropped to his knees. Molten metal poured freely from his wounds. Sumyr launched forward and swung for a deathblow, but his sword struck the ground that Fell had once occupied. The Under-King had simply disappeared into the surface of the mountain. Sumyr raged and his sword blazed, liquefying the stone beneath it. "I'll scorch this land into molten glass. Then where will you hide, Brother?"

Sumyr's taunts were interrupted as an arrow smashed into the side of his helm. Ullstag took aim at Sumyr and launched another arrow that banged loudly into the Fire King's crown with tremendous force, notching it. Sumyr stared at the Bearzyrk with his burning eye. "Time to burn, pale cub of Ghostmane!"

His sword ignited, and from it he hurled a ball of flame. The fire hurtled toward Ullstag and the Jadebow, striking their position. Cries filled the air, and the remaining archers of the Jadebow scattered. Lying in a heap of scorched bodies was the blackened form of Ullstag, badly burned but somehow still alive. He desperately tried to crawl away from the king of Firehome, but the giant of fire stood triumphantly above him.

"Bearzyrk, you seem to have many lives," Sumyr said, somewhat surprised. "You survived the watery doom at the lake, and now, the wrath of my fire . . . Well, since I can't drown or burn you, let us see how you fare with twenty feet of iron." King Sumyr towered over Ullstag and raised his sword, ready to make ruin of the fallen archer.

There was a loud twang followed by an angry buzzing sound that stopped the fire giant and turned his mocking laughter into screams of pain. A green, feathered arrow jutted forth from his eye socket, and Sumyr's rage became madness. The lord of Firehome was blind. Ullstag looked over to where the arrow had come from, and he saw a glorious sight that stirred his old heart with pride.

Ullyr stood tall and lean against the morning sky. And he was not alone, for in his left arm he held a magnificent set of golden antlers.

"Ullyr, Dawn Breaker sings beautifully this morning," Ullstag said proudly.

The Jadebow chieftain slowly limped forward and nocked another arrow with his teeth. With much effort he pushed his arm forward, and with his remaining strength, he readied for the killing shot.

"Watch out!" cried Ullstag.

Ullyr looked and saw a snarling fire giant charging at him from the south. Ullstag was too maimed to fight, and he helplessly watched the chieftain as he launched another arrow, skewering the giant in the chest.

The maddened Fire King howled and slashed blindly. Ullyr, slinging Dawn Breaker on his back, barely had time to grab the fallen Bearzyrk and pull him out of the deadly path of Sumyr's fiery blade. Both fell in a heap and lay still.

"You will all burn for this!" Sumyr screamed. Fire roared from his throat, sending columns of flame hurtling forward. Giant and Pandyr alike were consumed by the firestorm, and many who weren't were carved in two by the enraged swings of Sumyr's great iron sword. The king of Firehome was destroying everything in his madness. The very air was ablaze.

It was then that the battered Under-King returned to the fray. Though his wounds had healed somewhat, the fury of his brother's wrath had scarred his body. Regardless of the pain, Fell would not let his sister's children perish. With great effort, he sent a shockwave toward his brother, striking at the earth beneath the Fire King's iron boots, knocking him prone.

Silver rivulets ran like blood from the corner of his mouth, and the Under-King coughed weakly. "I am still here, Brother. Come, finish me if you can!" He stumbled into the mountainside, and it opened up for him, creating a gigantic tunnel. Fell limped into its depths, taunting his brother. "I see you, Brother! I'll be waiting for you."

"Face me, coward! Face me!" screamed the Fire King. He moved toward the Under-King's voice, followed by a throng of his elite guard. They entered the cave and moved forward into the depths of the Under Realm.

The cave sealed itself up, and the mountainside was silent.

CHAPTER 30
THE HAMMER FALLS

HE BATTLE WAS FURIOUS AND deadly for both sides, and while the Pandyr fought fiercely, their numbers were diminishing. In the center of the battlefield stood the unconquerable Hammerheart clan. Its chieftain, Thoryn, was a whirlwind of doom.

"Their numbers are too great for us to battle forever. We must stop the tide!" he shouted as he pointed his ancient hammer at Wintyr. "Kill the heart, and the body dies!"

His clansmen nodded in agreement.

"His skin is solid as a mountain. We'll need to get closer to strike a mortal blow . . . but how? Just being near him is death." Thoryn thought for a moment and reached into his tunic. He pulled forth the last of his magic honeycomb and devoured it. He looked to the others around him, and they all understood.

The Hammerheart warriors took what little honeycomb they had left and gave it to their chieftain, who swallowed it down by the handful. He gazed at his fellow clansmen, and his eyes were burning with the fire of Sprign's last gift.

He belched and smiled broadly before he turned around and charged at the lord of Icegard. Thoryn stopped not a hundred paces from Wintyr and

climbed to the top of a stone ledge. The honeycomb warmed his limbs with an amber fire, but through its radiant heat, he could still feel Wintyr's cold gnawing at his core. Even standing on the rock, the Hammerheart chieftain rose to a height that barely reached the icy chest of Wintyr.

He hurled not hammer but insults at the lord of Icegard. "Face my hammer, Lord Snowflake! I'm over here, you slack-eyed giantess! I've faced more danger dancing with my daughter!"

Lord Wintyr looked at the tiny Thoryn and laughed mockingly. The Hammerheart chieftain was no more than a fly next to him, standing defiantly on the stone precipice. "I am here, insignificant spawn of Sprign," he said as he opened his arms wide. "You wish to face me in single combat? Very well. You may strike at me first." He pounded his chest with an icy hand. Deadly spear-sized icicles rained down from his frozen beard, and they fell to the earth and smashed heavily on his frost-plated feet.

Thoryn noted a small area where the icy armor had cracked and revealed Wintyr's unprotected foot. Thoryn eyed the living glacier, and a grim smile split his lips.

The battlefield had quieted at the words of the Ice King. All that could be heard were the whirls of Thoryn's hammer and the laugh of Lord Wintyr. "Strike at me, little cub, and show my legions the might of Sprign's children!" bellowed the lord of Icegard.

Again, Thoryn smiled broadly and charged at the ice lord. At the very last instant, Thoryn leapt off of the cliff. Instead of hurling his mighty hammer, Thoryn hurtled downward nearly fifty feet before bringing his great-grandfather's hammer down furiously upon the ice lord's frost-shod foot.

The top of Wintyr's foot and a number of his toes shattered into a hundred shards as Thoryn's hammer broke clean through the living ice to strike the dark earth beneath. The ice lord reeled back and fell to the ground in a titanic heap. For the second time since creation, Lord Wintyr felt pain.

Thoryn was upon the fallen ice giant in an instant, and though he was nearly frozen, he whirled his hammer above his head fiercely. In a flashing arc, he brought it down upon the ice lord's chest, right above where the fiend's heart would be.

Ice flew in a thousand directions, and the hammer sang triumphantly.

Unfortunately, the cold of Wintyr had worked its way into Thoryn's body. Thoryn lurched forward and clutched at his chest, his noble heart slowing fearsomely.

A shadow loomed over Thoryn, and he looked up to see Wintyr's massive blue hand descending upon him, intent on smashing him like a bug against the giant's chest. Thoryn staggered away as best as his numb legs would allow, and the Hammerheart chieftain crashed into the ground in a heap, rolling to a stop. His clansmen raced to grab him from the freezing cold mist that was enveloping him as the Ice King unsteadily stood up.

"Stay back, fools!" yelled Thoryn. "You'll freeze solid!"

Though they tried desperately to press forward, the Hammerheart were unable to get through the freezing fog that surrounded the frost giant and their chieftain.

"Fall back, Hammerheart! Retreat and regroup. Your chieftain owes the gimp-footed king his shot," said Thoryn, facing Wintyr with clattering teeth and mocking laughter.

The icy beard that Wintyr had borne was gone, smashed to pieces. His chest looked like a fractured mirror with a web of cracks and fissures gracing the surface. From within, an evil blue light pulsed rhythmically. The Hammerheart chieftain fiercely looked to his clansmen. They stared in horror and hurled their hammers against the ice lord, but they bounced off of Wintyr and fell uselessly to the ground.

Lord Wintyr peered down at the ruin of his foot in disbelief and anger. He roared at Thoryn, who despite being nearly frozen solid, stood to face his foe.

"I've s-seen newborn c-cubs walk better than the likes of y-you."

Wintyr roared in pain as he brought up his smashed foot and held it over the trapped chieftain. With numb limbs, Thoryn raised his hammer and laughed through frosted lips. "Step to it, you one-eyed, one-footed—"

The ice lord brought down his broken foot upon Thoryn until it crunched deep into the earth.

CHAPTER 31

WHEN STONE AND FIRE COLLIDE

KING SUMYR STUMBLED AFTER his brother, and the Under-King continued his descent deeper and deeper into the Under Realm. The blind king was led by his elite guard, and for miles they pursued the Under-King. In the darkening depths, the mad king Sumyr continued his verbal assault upon his brother.

"Coward! Traitor!" he screamed. "Face me!"

They journeyed farther into the Under Realm until they came to a dead end. Sumyr and his guards turned around only to have the ceiling slam shut upon their exit. "Fools, you've led us into a trap!" bellowed the Fire King.

He lashed out with his blade and made a bloody wreck of one of his guardsmen. Sumyr shook with rage. His fiery crown and beard roared brightly at first, but they soon started to flicker and smoke. Sumyr clutched his chest as a spasm ripped through his body.

From the very walls around him came the words of the Under-King. "You are in my realm now, Brother," boomed the earthen voice.

Sumyr blindly attacked, striking out ferociously at the sound. His sword carved deep crevasses into the walls and the ground, melting stone with every strike. And with every swing, his fire dimmed.

"Your spark does not shine as bright in the Under Realm as it does in the world above. The hotter your rage, the more air you devour. And without air . . ."

King Sumyr frantically struck the walls, and from the damage poured gold and silver streams. As his fires dimmed, Sumyr toppled forward without even being struck. His burning crown clanked dully at the feet of the Under-King, who appeared out of the cavern wall. His body was wounded horribly. He slowly went toward his brother and sat beside the fallen Fire King.

"Brother, my fires die. As the fire dies, so do I—please!" begged the greatest of fire giants as he gasped for air.

The Under-King stared impassively at his brother, shaking his head. "No, Brother, it is time for you to leave the world . . . It is time for us both to leave . . . for now."

Silver and gold torrents poured from his wounds and pooled around the Under-King. Fell looked at the crown of Sumyr as the last of the fires winked into nothingness, leaving only a dull iron circlet. The Under-King rested quietly, and soon he sat as silent and as still as the stone he was once born from and had, at last, returned to.

***

High above in the upper world, the Pandyr and other denizens of Mistgard fought for their very existence. The giants attacked in disorganized waves, while the discipline of the Pandyr allowed them to stay alive against their enemies' crushing numbers.

The Storm Speaker stood atop the world, surveying the battle, and at his side were the Jadebow elders Ullyr and Ullstag. Both were burned by the fires of Sumyr, and though singed and beaten, they still had enough strength to stand.

Suddenly, the mighty battlements that protected the clans cracked and crumbled to dust. The primitive underkin of Fell stopped their attacks and stood motionless against the relentless giantkin swarm. Cries arose from the Pandyr as they watched their once-moving allies turn into lifeless stone.

"What magic is this?" exclaimed the Bearzyrk archer.

"'Tis no magic, Ullstag," said the Storm Speaker sadly. "It signifies the passing of the Under-King."

After a moment, Ullyr spoke. "Does that mean that the Fire King has won? Fell went into the earth with Sumyr, and both were swallowed by the mountain."

The Storm Speaker nodded his head toward the raging battle. Here and there, fire giants pitched forward or fell backward, leaving nothing but crumpled heaps of red ash and blackened armor. "Even in death, it seems the Under-King has defeated his brother. Still, we have lost a powerful ally in this battle."

"If we are of Sprign, why did we not die when she did?" said Ullstag. "Why did we not fall?"

"Sprign did not want slaves. When she created all of the creatures of Mistgard, she gave them free will to choose their own paths," said the Storm Speaker.

The Pandyr, seeing the army of fire giants destroyed, renewed their attacks, but the battle was far from won. More frost giants surged forth from the clouds below in an azure wave of doom and broke hard upon the Pandyr clans. Though the Pandyr fought with great discipline and skill, they were forced back time and time again as the tides of frost giants crushed down upon their lines. Their defenses were shattered, and soon there was no place left to fall back to. Wintyr strode forward with his vast army, relishing the extermination of his sister's creations.

The Storm Speaker stood defiantly atop his perch, with Ullyr and Ullstag and what remained of the broken and bloodied clans around him. It was here that they prepared for their final stand. Though hopelessly outnumbered, the Pandyr would give the lord of Icegard everything their bodies could give—everything but fear. They faced their foe united. Sunspear lances stood beside the stone mauls of the Hammerheart and the deadly arrows of the Jadebow. Thundermaw axes and Darkcloud clubs were joined by Mistcloak knives, Ironbeard swords, and Iceclaw gauntlets. The beasts of Mistgard stood proudly next to the clans. Horn and fang still had much to give to the battle.

Suddenly the Storm Speaker looked upon the field in horror as he saw Ursara was running wildly toward him. "No, Ursara! Do not come here. It is doom!" he shouted.

She ran as fast as she could, clutching something in her hands.

"Father . . . Father! It's Gloam! He has words for you!"

The Storm Speaker's voice cracked with fear. "No, Ursara, do not come here!"

For the first time in her life, Ursara ignored her father's words. She climbed shakily up the rocky precipice and ran to his arms.

"Daughter, listen to me—" he said, but he was cut off by his daughter's shout.

"Listen, Father! Listen to the words. I could only make out a few, but it sounded like he said—" She was drowned out by the long drone of a hunting horn. The Storm Speaker looked up and saw a shape—many shapes, in fact, dotting the edge of the clouds.

Gloam chittered feebly, and the Storm Speaker leaned down to the little bird and cupped his hands around his ears. He looked up and then smiled at Ursara.

Ursara's face was full of emotion. "Is it true?" she said.

The horn sounded again, and this time it was followed by a score more. From out of the mist charged a herd of phantom white spearhorn, and upon their backs were riders.

The Storm Speaker nodded. "Yes, Daughter."

They watched, along with the entirety of the Pandyr, as the ninth clan of Mistgard thundered up the slopes of the Aesirmyr and charged into the armies of the frost giants.

Ullstag nearly fell off of the ledge in amazement, once again being pulled to safety by the one-armed Ullyr. "It cannot be—the rider!" the Bearzyrk shouted.

The Jadebow chieftain looked toward the approaching warriors with his keen eye and spotted the large form of Frostvang, but he was not the rider leading the charge. At its head rode the largest Bearzyrk the Pandyr had ever seen, dwarfing even Ullstag in height and frame. The rider's long white mane flowed free in the frigid air, and gripped in his paws was a pair of glowing spears.

The Jadebow chieftain knew the answer and still could not believe what he was seeing. The Bearzyrk was clearly staggered by the sight as well. "Can it be? The rider appears to be—"

Lord Wintyr's roar cracked the sky, and his scream was the sound of a thousand glaciers shattering. He turned and faced his most hated enemy of all . . .

"*Ghostmane!*"

CHAPTER 32

THE CHARGE OF
THE BEARZYRK

THE PANDYR WERE AMAZED AT the strength of the Bearzyrk's charge. They split the center of the frost giant army, cleaving a frosty path of carnage. Spearhorn and stone axe gored and ripped in tandem, and at the front was the mighty Ghostmane. Crimson death and cobalt fury stabbed at the giants, and each one who approached crumpled to the ground.

Lord Wintyr stormed forward and smashed into the Bearzyrk, crushing and freezing his ancient enemies. The broken clans of the Pandyr watched the valorous charge of their lost clansmen, which ignited their battle lust once again; they rallied and surged into the fray. The frost of Wintyr slowed them little as their blood came alive with battle fire. Black and white stood back-to-back with ghost and gray, and both Pandyr and Bearzyrk pounded the Ice King's army with savage fury.

The Jadebow rained mayhem down upon the giants' front, while the Iceclaw and Ironbeard surrounded the foe and attacked the giants from the rear. The Storm Speaker was alive with hope and commanded the storms from atop the rocky pinnacle, launching emerald thunderbolts at the giants' center. All the clans were engaged in what had to be the greatest battle the mountain island of Mistgard had ever witnessed.

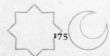

Ursara fetched quiver after quiver of arrows for both Ullyr and Ullstag, who sent them forth as fast as she procured them. Far below, the Storm Speaker saw Frostvang and a group of Bearzyrk locked in battle with the frost giant host. The Pandyr sent down rapid arcs of brilliant death upon the blue fiends and splintered them to shards of ice. The old Bearzyrk saluted the Storm Speaker and barreled off into another melee.

From across the battlefield, the lord of Icegard's voice boomed again. "Ghostmane . . . Come forth and die!" he roared in fury.

This time, he got an answer from the Bearzyrk in the form of a blue-bladed spear hurled into his empty eye socket. The force snapped Wintyr's head back so far that it touched between his broad, icy shoulders.

"I return what was once yours, frost fiend," said Ghostmane.

Momentarily stunned, the lord of Icegard bellowed with rage and then wantonly hurtled forward toward the Bearzyrk army, viciously swinging down his axe. Finally he saw his foe before him. Ghostmane sat atop his great spear-horn, statue-like, his crimson spear glowing brightly. Wintyr chopped down with his heavy blade as Ghostmane moved with surprising speed and struck at the Ice King's legs. The flaming Eye of Fire scarred the icy limbs but could not find a weak spot behind knee or ankle. Wintyr pulled the spear from his empty eye socket and swung his weapon ferociously into the armies of the Pandyr and the Bearzyrk. They fell before his fury by the score. Ghostmane charged again from behind and struck with the Eye of Fire. The burning spear cut but failed to penetrate the icy crust that protected the ice lord's body.

The Storm Speaker watched in dismay. Calling upon the elements of sky, wind, and rain, the Storm Speaker bent the surging clouds below to his will and sent a glimmering bolt of fury that crashed into the Ice King, causing him to momentarily forget the Bearzyrk and focus his attention on where the Storm Speaker perched.

The Storm Speaker quickly retreated, calling for his friends to follow. They hastily beat a path down the rocky pinnacle just in time to avoid being cleaved in two by the blade of the Ice King. Seething with rage, Lord Wintyr whirled menacingly back and forth, looking for the Bearzyrk or his storm-wielding ally.

Finally, through the mists, he saw the Storm Speaker and Ursara assisting the wounded Ullyr and Ullstag. Father and daughter bore their weight as best they could and helped them run as swiftly as their broken bodies would allow them to. Wintyr smiled coldly and raised his axe as the frantic Storm Speaker

urged his daughter forward. "Run, child! I'll take Ullyr and Ullstag! Go!"

"I'll not leave you, Father. I'll stay with you until it's over."

They looked over their shoulders as the gigantic shadow of Wintyr loomed over them, but their eyes were drawn not to the giant's wicked face but to the remnants of their ruined stone pinnacle.

"Wintyr . . ."

The Ice King's eyes left the scrambling figures of Ursara and the Storm Speaker and fell upon the rocky precipice that he had smashed mere moments ago. Though most of the ledge had crumbled to the earth, there still stood one jagged stone, atop which sat his most hated of enemies.

Ghostmane leapt high into the air, spear in hand, and crashed down upon Lord Wintyr's chest. It was here that he struck with the Eye of Fire. The glowing spear burned into the weakened chest plate of the ice lord, and Wintyr bellowed as it sank deep. Where Thoryn's mighty hammer had smashed, Ghostmane's spear took advantage. The spear's tip burned a crimson path toward the heart of Wintyr.

The Bearzyrk clan battled fiercely upon the blood-soaked ground of the Aesirmyr. If the murderous voice that urged the Bearzyrk to kill spoke to them that day, it was put to good use. The armies clashed, and both sides took heavy losses. With the defeat of the fire giants and their king, and with the arrival of the Bearzyrk, the tide had turned to the clans' favor. The Pandyr broke the disorganized blue surge of frost fiends, hurling them off the mountain and into the mists below. Cheers went up here and there, but they were soon interrupted by primal howls and curses.

Ghostmane clung desperately to the Eye of Fire and thrust it forward again, pushing it deeper and deeper into the lord of Icegard. Wintyr raged and twisted madly, finally managing to grip the Bearzyrk and wrench him by his torso. The motion snapped the shaft of the flaming spear in half, and Wintyr laughed wickedly.

Ghostmane made a desperate grab and snagged the burning spear haft, freeing it from his enemy's chest. The crimson blade reflected luridly on the skin of Wintyr. The lord of Icegard spoke triumphantly as the tiny Ghostmane struggled feebly in his crushing grip. "Today, Mistgard will perish, but you will die first!"

Wintyr opened his mouth impossibly wide and swallowed Ghostmane whole.

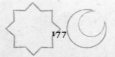

CHAPTER 33
AT THE HEART
OF WINTYR

FAR BELOW, A GUTTURAL CRY escaped from the Bearzyrk clansmen, who watched in horror as Ghostmane disappeared into the hoary mouth of Wintyr. The entire clan fell to the ground, trying desperately to stand. The loss of their most venerable ancestor, who hours ago had returned to them from the past, brought forth the horrible change that was the curse of their kind. Hatred and rage flowed freely in their contorting forms.

The giants, seeing their enemies racked with pain, laughed and launched into them. Icy blades stabbed into fur and flesh. Unfortunately for the giants, this had little effect. The Bearzyrk seemed immune to the damage, though many of the wounds they bore were mortal. Weapons fell from their clawed grasp, their hands no longer capable of holding anything as complex as a handle. A primordial fury ran through the Bearzyrk, and with the snapping of bone, their claws and fangs sprang out, jaws unhinged horrifically, and figures that were once Bearzyrk rose up and tore viciously at their enemy.

They charged forward on four limbs like beasts, no longer aware of the frost giants. They mowed through them and swept them aside like chaff. They hurtled ahead recklessly and crashed their might upon the body of Wintyr, tearing through ice and frost with bloody claws and jagged fangs.

181

Swinging his weapon like a scythe, the ice lord dashed the beasts to and fro, bending bones and snapping spines. The maddened beast once called Frostvang climbed atop the bodies of his fallen kinsmen and hurled himself upon the ice lord, raking across icy plates with his claws.

For all the savaging that was brought upon the body of Wintyr, none could penetrate his frigid frame. With the attack faltering, it seemed that whatever gains the Pandyr had made when the Bearzyrk first appeared had been lost. The frost giants rallied against the outnumbered clansmen, while the Bearzyrk, mad with grief, continued their futile attacks against the Ice King. The Bearzyrk perished one by one, till all who remained were Frostvang and a score of his Long Coats. They drew together and prepared for a final assault.

The Ice King laughed and gloated in his victory. "Ghostmane is dead, and soon his pathetic cubs will join him. The spirit of Sprign will weep frozen tears tonight." A baleful wind sang coldly in the air as Wintyr looked at his armies that had surrounded the last of the Pandyr and the Bearzyrk. "Today, sons of Icegard, Mistgard shall fall!"

The giants bellowed in fiendish pleasure as the axe of their great king rose high in the sky, blotting out the golden skull's light. From deep inside the fractured chest of the Ice King, a strange purple light glowed dimly. Wintyr's body was struck by an invisible force. The jolt shook him from head to shattered foot. He dropped his axe and clutched at his chest. A horrific splitting sound emanated loudly in the cold air. The sound came from inside the Ice King.

The light inside Wintyr, once dim, now grew in strength and beamed through the king's splintered breast, sending out brilliant purple rays. A spasm racked Wintyr as if he were being torn apart from within.

"No! *Nooooo!*" he screamed.

That day, the frost giants heard a sound come from their king that they had never heard before.

It was the sound of fear.

Wintyr tore at his mouth and shoved his fingers deep into his gaping maw, but to no avail. He clutched and pounded at his chest, and a fearful cry slipped forth from icy blue lips. A terrific ringing sound split the din of the morning. Wintyr's gleaming blue eye rolled back into his skull, and the king of the frost giants wavered on his heels, trying desperately to stay up.

"Grab the wounded and fall back!" yelled the Storm Speaker.

Pandyr and Bearzyrk alike grabbed their fallen and pulled them as far back as they could, dodging the crushing footfalls of the enormous frost giant.

Ursara yelled to the Storm Speaker, "Father, look!"

The Storm Speaker followed her gaze. There, piercing the icy chest of Wintyr, was the glowing red tip of a spearhead. It gleamed brightly against Wintyr's azure skin like a single drop of fiery blood. With brutal force, the spearhead was pushed farther and farther out until, finally, it burst forth in a spray of ice. Lord Wintyr looked down at the last thing that he would see: a glowing red-bladed spear and, clutching it, a large white paw.

Wintyr stumbled backward and fell helplessly upon the ground, trapping a score or more of his own beneath his enormous body—not that the frost giants felt it. As the king of Icegard fell dead, so, too, did his minions. Where once stood vile and screaming fiends of living frost, there now lay nothing but mounds of foul-smelling ice.

The Pandyr approached the body of Wintyr, whose gaze was fixed blankly at the Skulls in the Sky, a look of confusion forever etched into his frozen visage.

"The fiend's heart still beats. Listen," said Ullstag, drawing back an arrow.

"There is a heart that pounds from within the body of Wintyr, but it is not a heart born in Icegard," said the Storm Speaker.

The pounding continued for a few more seconds until, from out of the center of Wintyr's chest, a familiar figure burst forth. Shards of ice coated his white fur, and the figure staggered from the body of the Ice King. Upon his ninth step, he stopped and fell to the ground.

He lay next to the lord of the frost giants, looking up at the sky with icy blue eyes. The stormy winds of Wintyr gave one final gust, blowing aside the giant furs that wrapped the figure's body. A faint whisper could be heard from him.

"Ursara?"

"Frostpaw!" she yelled as she rushed to his side. The Storm Speaker and the others gathered around the fallen boy.

"By Sprign," said Ullstag, scratching his head.

It was indeed Frostpaw. Upon his large frame hung the skin of the great Ghostmane, and in his hand was a broken spear, the Eye of Fire. Its flames flickered out, and the blade turned to black iron.

Ursara held his head in her arms. Frostpaw was deathly cold to the touch and shook tremendously. "Frostpaw . . . Frostpaw! Father, do something!" she cried helplessly.

The Storm Speaker was by her side, and he looked at the boy with a smile.

Tears streamed down Ursara's face and fell upon Frostpaw's, freezing immediately. He feebly raised his hand to her neck and touched the necklace he had made for her. Frostpaw smiled at Ursara, then slowly closed his eyes. She looked down and touched the necklace she had given him. Through all the battles and hardships, it still rested snugly around his wrist.

"Wherever you go, my heart goes with you, Frostpaw."

Frostvang bulled through the Pandyr, but he hardly looked like the old Bearzyrk they had known earlier. He lumbered heavily on all fours; his coat was clawed and torn, and he bore many grievous wounds. His eyes still burned with intelligence, but his body had regressed to that of a primal beast. Fangs and horns jutted from jaw and skull, and he sniffed the fallen boy.

In words thick and primitive, he spoke. "Ghostmane killed many, but it was Frostpaw who killed Wintyr. Your love kept him warm. He died a good death."

Ursara put her arms around Frostvang's massive head and cried into his mane. The Storm Speaker was quiet. He walked over to the body of his son and stood for a few moments, rubbing his beard.

"I would have to disagree with you, old friend. For a good death, surely one must die."

This startled both Frostvang and Ursara out of their grief, and they looked up, confused. Ursara turned toward her father. "But he's not breathing, Father. I felt his last breath upon my face," she said with tear-filled eyes.

"Watch closely now . . ."

Many moments passed, and just as Ursara was about to lose her mind, she saw something.

Frostpaw's chest rose slowly.

Ursara knelt over Frostpaw, placing her ear on his chest. She waited again for what seemed like an eternity, and just as she was going to attribute what she saw to her eyes cruelly teasing her, she heard a faint heartbeat. She took Frostpaw's cold hand in hers and looked at his wrist. There, within the heart stone, a distant red glimmer danced. She turned to the Storm Speaker and the gathered clansmen. "How is this possible, Father?" she said softly.

The Storm Speaker put his arms around his daughter and held her. "He wore the skin of the greatest of all Bearzyrk. Perhaps that was the reason, or maybe it was his love for you, my daughter. Maybe the freezing temperatures that dwelled in Wintyr's body preserved him from death, leaving him in a deep sleep." The Storm Speaker's voice hitched in his throat as he lifted Frostpaw to his chest and wept. "I do not know the answer for this, and for the first time in my nine hundred and ninety-nine years, I am fine without knowing the answer. I am just happy that my son is alive."

HAMMERHEART

CHAPTER 34

THROUGH FROST
AND FIRE

HE BATTLE OF MISTGARD WAS OVER.

The giants were defeated, and the children of Sprign lived. But there was little time to celebrate. The following days were spent burying the dead and healing the wounded.

The Hammerheart grieved tremendously at the loss of their brave leader. When his body was dug from the snow, they found him still clutching his hammer with a frozen smile upon his face.

As Thoryn had lived, so had he died.

No matter how much the Hammerheart were asked, they refused to bury their chieftain atop the Aesirmyr with the rest of the fallen. He would follow them back down the mountain to their homeland and sleep in the Circle in the Sky, where his fathers and grandfathers slept.

The storms that raged below the Aesirmyr dissipated, and the Pandyr were finally able to start their long journey home.

The other creatures of Mistgard returned to their lands as well. The old jaegyr hound Fenryr and his pack were the last to leave the Pandyr, looking back to the clans and offering a round of howls for the fallen. After their song, they raced off and faded into the mists.

As the Pandyr made the trek down the Aesirmyr, they were horrified with what they saw. Trees were blackened and twisted by the fires that had raged through the forests. The ice storms had turned the earth to frigid, lifeless rock. Nothing had been spared from the devastation.

Days later, when the clans approached the Tundyr, they were amazed to see that the great frozen lakes had melted and were choked with icebergs and fallen trees. The Bearzyrk homelands were in ruins.

The Storm Speaker spoke quietly to his daughter as they approached the Den of the Slayers, or what was left of it. "The Bearzyrk need us, Ursara," he said worriedly. "Their bodies and minds are wounded, and their lands are ruined. I believe that when we return to our lands, we will find the same thing. I cannot be in two places at once and—"

"I'll stay here with the Bearzyrk, Father," she said, smiling. Through the whole trip down the mountain, Ursara had ridden with Frostpaw on a litter pulled by a massive spearhorn. "The Bearzyrk gave up so much to help us, and it is the least we can do to repay them for their sacrifices. I will help them heal, and when they are healed, I will help them rebuild."

The Storm Speaker hugged his daughter and kissed her gently on her forehead. Overhead, the great albatross, Fog, soared high. "I'll be checking in on you from time to time."

Gloam landed on her shoulder and cheeped into her ear. "And we will be checking in on you, too, Father. Someone needs to make sure you eat and sleep enough."

Frostvang and Ullstag approached, and they, too, said their goodbyes to the Storm Speaker and their new clansmen.

"Farewell, little chieftain," said Ullstag, wrapping his arms around Ullyr in a great hug.

Ullyr gave the Bearzyrk a hug back as best as he could with his remaining arm. "Thank you, Ullstag. We thank you for everything." Ullyr unslung Dawn Breaker from his back and held it up to the Bearzyrk.

Smiling, Ullstag patted the bow fondly and lumbered over to the warriors of the Hammerheart clan.

"Your chieftain drank with us, and he fought with us, and he even died with us. It will be known to all that the noble son of the Hammerheart toppled the lord of Icegard with a single blow! The Bearzyrk will forever remember him in our stories."

The Storm Speaker bade farewell to the Bearzyrk and then walked over to his son, who lay still and silent, covered in the skin of Ghostmane. *Goodbye, my boy. When you wake up, I will be there to welcome you back. Until then, sleep well.* He touched his son's brow and felt the freezing chill of Wintyr that clung to his face.

The Pandyr continued down the mountain. Snow and ice covered the land but were slowly melting away. Like the clansmen's wounds, Mistgard, too, would need some time to heal.

The Pandyr traveled many miles, always under the watchful Skulls in the Sky. With every day, the skulls grew closer and closer.

Soon, they will unite, thought the Storm Speaker.

CHAPTER 35

THE END BEGINS

EEKS LATER, THE PANDYR FINALLY returned to their ancestral homes. There was no parade to welcome them, and the only arms that reached up to greet them were the broken and blackened beams of their once-magnificent halls. Few structures were left standing. Around the Circle in the Sky, the stone totems that once stood watch lay toppled and ravaged. The parents of the children left in the care of the Under-King, Fell, were beyond lost with grief. With Fell gone, there was no way to reach their cubs, and amidst the ruins, mothers and fathers grieved silently for their little ones. The clans worked furiously, but try as they might, they could not break through the mountainside where the children were trapped.

The following days were bleak and dreary. The land was devastated; nothing grew or bloomed. No scent of grass or pine floated in the wind, and the trees were stripped bare like rotted skeletons. High above the blight, Fog and the Storm Speaker surveyed the lifeless world.

"Without Sprign, Mistgard dies," said the Storm Speaker. He guardedly looked high overhead at the giant, staring skulls. "And the joining of the skulls is soon to come."

He guided Fog down and dismounted from Traveler, who futilely searched for grass to forage. The Storm Speaker rested his hand upon his mount. "Fog, tell Ursara it is time to gather the clans. Let the nine clans stand together one last time." With a screech, Fog rose high into the clouds and disappeared from sight.

The Storm Speaker moved about the remnants of the clans, helping where he could, consoling grieving parents and tending to the wounded. The clans had grown close during the battle and the days that followed. Upon returning, they had worked together to clean up the refuse and to search for anything that could help them survive.

In the following days, Ursara and the Bearzyrk arrived, and father and daughter were reunited. It felt as if it had been years since he had held his girl.

"You look well, Father. You've been sleeping?" said Ursara.

The Storm Speaker laughed. "A little bit." He looked at the beasts that were once the indomitable Bearzyrk. "How fares the ninth clan?"

She smiled sadly. "There is little left of them. Most can no longer communicate as they once did, and they tend to wander the lakes and mountains, hunting and searching for food. Fewer and fewer return every night. The kinship they shared seems lost. Now they prefer to be alone." The Storm Speaker's head fell in grief, and his daughter put her tiny hand on his. "Still, there is some hope. Not all were as devastated by the change. Ullstag seems hardly affected, and he has busied himself repairing the Den of the Slayers," said Ursara with a slight smile.

"And Frostvang?" said the Storm Speaker grimly.

Ursara's smile faded, and though it did not completely leave, it bore a touch of sorrow again. "Frostvang lives, though not the way we knew him before. He can speak, but with much difficulty. I feel it is only a matter of time before he, too, is lost to us."

"And what of Frostpaw?" said the Storm Speaker.

His daughter smiled wanly.

They looked to the sky, where the ever-present skulls loomed overhead, nearly on top of each other. The Storm Speaker held Ursara tenderly and stroked her brow.

Behind them, Traveler wandered in the Circle in the Sky, looking on the frozen ground for anything suitable to eat. She stopped abruptly when she found a particular patch of earth, and she prodded it with her hoof. Leaning down, the gray elkhorn started nibbling at something with interest.

The Storm Speaker walked over and knelt down, moving his mount aside, much to Traveler's protests. He looked at his daughter and smiled. "The coming night will bring many things, but I have a feeling in my bones that they are not as bad as we think."

Ursara moved to the spot of earth that Traveler had seemed so occupied with moments ago. She knelt down and looked at the hard ground, scanning for anything that would hold her father's attention.

By her feet, jutting through the lifeless ground, sprouted little blades of grass.

***

Together for the first time in many thousands of years, the great Skulls in the Sky touched, and the golden skull joined with its silver twin. The union cast an ever-growing reddish light upon the island of Mistgard.

The Storm Speaker and Ursara went to join the nine clans of Mistgard, not with heavy hearts but with hope. A slight breeze blew from the east, rustling the Storm Speaker's beard, and with it came the faintest of scents, which caused the Storm Speaker to smile. Ursara looked at her father and wondered if she was going mad.

"Father, is that what . . ."

The Storm Speaker nodded. "Yes, Daughter. The wind smells of honey-pine. Soon, the end begins."

CHAPTER 36

A REUNION
OF SORTS

THE NINE CLANS DID NOT SPEND the day in fear or in solitude
but united.

What little food they had stored was brought out and eaten.
One of the clans had found that their mead cellars had been
untouched by the ravages of the giant hordes, hidden under fallen
timber and scorched beam. At the mention of mead, the clansmen had made
short work of the heavy logs and swept away the debris as easily as if it had
been sweat from their brow. Iceclaw and Ironbeard drank with Mistcloak and
Darkcloud. Hammerheart jested and grappled with Thundermaw over who
had the strongest clansmen. Jadebow and Bearzyrk sat with Sunspear, and
they spoke in reverent tones about the losses their clans bore.

After many cups and boasts, Ullstag and Ullyr challenged each other to
archery contests, each splitting the other's arrows in twain till their quivers
were empty. The Hammerheart gave toasts to their chieftain's name and to
his mighty hammer, which sat on an elevated shield at the head of their table.
The revelry continued under the reddish light, and all the while, the Storm
Speaker stood with Ursara and Frostvang, quietly watching the sky.

"The union nears its end, my friends. Look!" said the Storm Speaker as
he pointed his spear toward the skulls.

The crowds grew silent as the moment approached. The skulls broke free from each other, and the earth rumbled, knocking over tables and beds. Instead of running madly and succumbing to fear, the Pandyr held their friends and loved ones, reciting the words of their people. *"By tooth and by claw, by fang and by paw."* They recited the words again and again. Unafraid, they waited for whatever would happen next. And they waited together.

The rumbling continued for many minutes. Ullstag took up a fallen horn of mead and drank down what was left. "I expected the end of the world would be a bit more climactic than this," he mumbled through frothy lips.

After some time, the rumbling stopped, and something that had been missing from the clans for what seemed like years drifted to the ears of the Pandyr.

It was the magical choir of children's laughter.

The beautiful noise caused many to rush, heedless of danger, toward the sound.

From over the hills that surrounded the Circle in the Sky came a throng of small figures. They saw the Pandyr and began yelling and running toward them with wild abandon.

"Papa!"

"Mama!"

The children of the Pandyr had returned home.

The Pandyr raced toward the children, calling their names, and in moments, the lost cubs ran into the loving arms of their mothers and fathers. Cries of happiness soared through the air, and embraces were given and accepted.

As the Pandyr rejoined their children, another sound drifted over the hill. It was the sound of an infant crying. Fearing that one of their children was hurt, the Pandyr ran up the hill to look down upon the Circle in the Sky.

In the center was the newly risen tomb of Sprign, and atop the stone wailed a small baby.

As the Pandyr approached, they noticed other strange things as well. Upon the ground were sprigs of fresh green grass and moss. From the dead trunks of blackened trees, young saplings rose up toward the sky. A low buzz filled the air as fat bees drifted lazily about the Circle in the Sky.

The Storm Speaker walked toward the tomb, careful not to step on anything.

"What's going on, Father?" said Ursara quietly.

The Storm Speaker approached the small child. The baby was crying, but she stopped as she looked up at the giant Storm Speaker. She was a little thing; her skin was pale green, and her emerald hair gleamed brightly. Her eyes were very large and amber in color, like rich honey. Atop her head sprouted a small pair of curved horns. She raised her arms as the Storm Speaker bent to pick her up.

Ursara blinked in disbelief. "It—she's—"

The Storm Speaker smiled at his daughter.

"You knew, didn't you?" she blurted out.

"I had an idea. And, yes, Daughter, I believe she is." He turned and beckoned the Pandyr. "Come round, everyone! There is someone I must reintroduce you to," he said cheerfully.

Traveler sniffed at the little girl, and she giggled and touched the elkhorn's velvety fur. The Storm Speaker watched the clansmen gather round and gape at the baby, who cooed and reached her tiny hands into the air as if trying to catch the clouds.

"Pandyr and Bearzyrk of Mistgard, I would like you all to say hello . . . to Sprign."

CHAPTER 37

THE CYCLE BEGINS

HE PANDYR LOOKED AT THE Storm Speaker in wonder and disbelief. Ullyr came forward, eyeing the little one.

"Storm Speaker, how is this possible?" said the one-eyed Jadebow.

"It is simple, Chieftain. When Sprign left our world, there was an imbalance that needed to be rectified. Without Sprign's blessings to bring life back after Wintyr, Mistgard would die. The oldest stories of our kind tell us that the Skulls in the Sky joined to create the giants at the beginning of time. When they saw that the world was in chaos, they came together again to bring Sprign back."

"But with the deaths of Wintyr and Sumyr, will there not be an imbalance as well?" said Modyr, chieftain of the Darkcloud.

The Storm Speaker looked at the Darkcloud chieftain with a calm but serious face. "Aye, there would be. It would not surprise me to hear that the sounds of newborn cries fill the morning air in Icegard and Firehome as well."

"Are you telling me that after all the war and death, Wintyr and Sumyr live again?" said the Jadebow chieftain.

This did not sit well with the Pandyr. The Storm Speaker did his best to quiet them. "There cannot be one without the other. Day and night, Sprign and Wintyr, Sumyr and Fell, life and death—hush now," he said, looking down at Sprign. "The little Den Mother sleeps."

Sprign was nestled in the Storm Speaker's arm, curled amongst his flowing beard. When Ullyr spoke, it was in a hushed tone.

"Well, what are we to do with her now, Storm Speaker?"

The Storm Speaker looked over at Ullyr and smiled. "We will teach her. We will teach her everything she taught us."

He had started to walk away when Ursara called to him. "Father, I think we have forgotten something."

"What is it, child?" said the Storm Speaker.

Ursara held in her hands what appeared to be a rough-hewn boulder. She gave her father a strange smile. "There cannot be one without the other."

The rock uncurled into what looked like an infant made of stone. Small quartz crystals fell from eyes of amethyst, and a cry escaped a crevice that seemed to be a mouth. The sound it produced was a tiny rumble.

"Ah, yes, how could I have forgotten?" said the Storm Speaker.

The infant Under-King cried a seismic wail, and it seemed there was nothing to placate him with until a voice from behind them got their attention.

"Maybe you can give him this." The young daughter of the Hammerheart, Thorgrid, gently removed something from Sprign's tomb and walked over to the Storm Speaker. What she held in her hand was a small, lovingly made doll crafted to look like Sprign.

"I think he may want this," she said.

The Storm Speaker handed little Fell the doll, and he instantly stopped his crying and stared at it as though it were long-lost friend. He spoke in a strange earthen tongue, and the fallen obelisks in the Circle in the Sky rose back to their rightful places. Sprign's tomb fell apart. The slabs that once bore the body of his older sister rose up, and crude figures were birthed out of the stone. They moved slowly around the Storm Speaker and Ursara.

"Easy, Daughter. They have come for their king."

The stone golems held out what looked like arms, and they stood waiting. Ursara handed the little king to his minions and watched as they moved to the center of the Circle in the Sky. The underkin stopped at the command of the Under-Prince. He looked back at his sister and the Storm Speaker, and then he and his minions disappeared into the earth with a rumble.

Thorgrid, looking very distraught, tugged gently on the Storm Speaker's cloak. "Storm Speaker, I can't find my father. Do you know where my father is?" Tears fell freely down her face. "He's dead, isn't he?"

A wave of sadness passed over the Storm Speaker. As much as it was a time of celebration for some, for many more, it was also a time of mourning. "Aye, little Hammerheart. I will tell you what happened to your father. And though sad, it is a great tale . . ."

The Storm Speaker walked with Thorgrid, Ursara, and the young Sprign. His words grew soft as they went over the hill, disappearing into the morning mist. "Your father stood against the lord of Icegard, alone and unafraid. With one swing of his mighty hammer, Thoryn, chieftain of the Hammerheart, heralded the beginning of the end of Wintyr."

A gentle rain fell from the sky, warm and clean. Emerald grass sprouted from mist-covered earth. Wintyr's wrath was over, and Sprign's time had come.

THE FIRST WINTER

HE FIRST SNOWFALL WAS neither as harsh nor as violent as it had been during the war, or as it would be in years to come. For the time being, it was just a soft white powder that dusted the landscape and covered it with a blanket of tiny jewels.

The island of Mistgard was alive this morning with much commotion and revelry, for it was a day of great celebration. The nine clans of Mistgard gathered around the newly rebuilt Thunder's Home to see the cubs of the Storm Speaker's daughter.

Not only were the clans assembled, but so, too, were the herds of elkhorn and the numerous other fauna of Mistgard. Even the old Fenryr had come with his pack of jaegyr hounds and bounding pups to witness the day's events. The crowds quieted as the Storm Speaker walked out of the doorway alongside the young giantess Sprign.

She had grown tall and lean, and though she was not even a year in age, she came up to the Storm Speaker's chest. Following the Storm Speaker and Sprign lumbered old Frostvang, who, on all fours, rumbled at the throng of guests to move aside. Sitting atop the back of the great Bearzyrk was Ursara, and in her arms she cradled two cubs. The Storm Speaker walked by her side and put his arm around her, beaming.

Ursara looked from her father to the gathered clans. "Clansmen and companions of Mistgard, I thank you for joining my father and me today. It would not be the same without you—without all of you."

The Storm Speaker looked at the crowd and marveled. The clans of Mistgard were no longer in danger of annihilation, and it pleased the Storm Speaker that they had not gone back to their feuding ways. "We are all the children of Sprign now." He gazed down at the little giantess, who smiled back at him.

"And she is now a child of the clans." Ursara finished thanking the gathered crowd, and then she introduced the newest members of her family. "Friends, I'd like you all to meet Frostmane and Shadowpaw."

The Pandyr cheered at the sight of the cubs of Ursara and Frostpaw.

One of the cubs surprised the clansmen, not for being Wintyr-Born but for being the first female Bearzyrk. Frostmane's fur was ghostly white, and she had a mop of hair on her head that was as pale as the snow at the Pandyr's feet. Like all Wintyr-Born, she was large for her age and bore a pair of brilliant blue eyes. She gave a small roar before turning back to her skin of honeyed milk.

The second cub was unlike anything the clansmen had seen before. Whereas his sister was white and pale, Shadowpaw's coat was as black as the night was dark. Born minutes after Frostmane, he was decidedly larger in size and had eyes the color of golden fire.

The dark coloring did not strike fear into the clansmen as it once might have done. Their old prejudices had dissipated after the battle with the giants. They were all children of Mistgard: the Pandyr, the Wintyr-Born, and those who would become known as the Fire-Born. In the years that followed, the birth of a Fire-Born would be held in high esteem, for the Fire-Born's strength surpassed even that of the mighty Bearzyrk.

The clansmen gathered around and gave gifts and tributes to the cubs. Tiny bows were given by Ullyr and his Jadebow. Little Thorgrid and the Hammerheart gave the newborns small dolls of Sprign and stone pendants carved in the shape of Thoryn's hammer. As the skulls set, the clans were welcomed into Thunder's Home for a grand feast. Mead was served by the barrel, and Ullstag himself had at least two. Much of the night was spent in revelry and telling tales of bravery, including the story of Thoryn facing Wintyr and the saga of Frostpaw and Ghostmane.

At the end of that tale, Ursara bade the party farewell, her cubs sleeping in her arms. As she ascended the stairs, Frostmane woke first, followed by her brother, Shadowpaw. "You two do everything together, don't you?" Ursara said.

The cubs quietly stared at their mother. Eyes of ice and fire looked up at her with heavy lids, and Ursara watched as her children drifted back to sleep. She took them to her room and laid them down on the thick quilt on the bed. "Rest now, my little cubs. We have a long journey tomorrow, and there is someone I want you to meet."

Ursara lay next to her cubs and watched as they slept. She lovingly touched a carved wooden heart that hung from a braid around her neck. Ursara closed her eyes, and she dreamt of a frozen land and the heart that beat beneath its surface.

***

Morning came to the Tundyr, the land of frozen lakes and plains. At its heart rested the Den of the Slayers. The war had caused much damage, but many of the inner halls had remained safe from harm. It was in these ancient halls that the bodies of the greatest heroes of the Bearzyrk rested. There they slept in cold and silent darkness, all but one. In the deepest hall, there was a light upon the walls, a light that shone a deep ruby red. Three tiers graced the hall, and atop the tiers were thrones of ancient make, all but one.

On the highest tier, a grand throne had been formed from living pine wrapped intricately around the broken remnants of an old seat of ice. Upon this throne sat a large Bearzyrk youth. He wore little more than a loincloth and an ancient skin upon his shoulders. The skin he wore was as ghostly white as his own, and on his lap rested a broken spear with a blade that once gleamed like a flame. Upon the walls danced the brilliant red light, which pulsed like the beating of a heart. The light emanated from a small heart-shaped stone fastened to the wrist of the youth. The pulse was slow at first but soon quickened in pace. The light that radiated from the charm also grew in intensity and power, and the room became warm. The frosty air turned to mist, and soon the walls of the chamber dripped with rivulets of icy sweat. The heat of the stone coursed through the body upon the throne, wrapping it in a warm embrace. The figure opened his eyes, and a smile crossed the face of the young Bearzyrk.

Frostpaw would meet his cubs today.

Dedicated to little Sophia, the one who started it all.

ACKNOWLEDGMENTS

The creator of this tale would like to raise a horn of Sprign's mead to the gods of thunder: Abbath, Amon Amarth, Demonaz, Cradle of Filth, Immortal, HammerFall, Judas Priest, Quorthon, Rush, Savatage, The Gates of Slumber, Visigoth, and the Kings of Metal: ManOwaR.

INSIGHT
EDITIONS

PO Box 3088
San Rafael, CA 94912
www.insighteditions.com

f Find us on Facebook: www.facebook.com/InsightEditions
🐦 Follow us on Twitter: @insighteditions

Copyright © 2017 Samwise Didier

Published by Insight Editions, San Rafael, California, in 2017. All rights reserved. No part
of this book may be reproduced in any form without written permission from the publisher.

Library of Congress Cataloging-in-Publication Data available.

ISBN: 978-1-60887-924-3

Publisher: Raoul Goff
Associate Publisher: Vanessa Lopez
Art Director: Chrissy Kwasnik
Designers: Jon Glick and Yousef Ghorbani
Managing Editor: Alan Kaplan
Project Editor: Greg Solano
Production Editor: Elaine Ou
Production Manager: Alix Nicholaeff
Production Assistant: Pauline Kerkhove Sellin

ROOTS of PEACE 🌳 REPLANTED PAPER

Insight Editions, in association with Roots of Peace, will plant two trees for each tree used in the
manufacturing of this book. Roots of Peace is an internationally renowned humanitarian organization
dedicated to eradicating land mines worldwide and converting war-torn lands into productive farms
and wildlife habitats. Roots of Peace will plant two million fruit and nut trees in Afghanistan and
provide farmers there with the skills and support necessary for sustainable land use.

Manufactured in China by Insight Editions

10 9 8 7 6 5 4 3 2 1